A Light Blazes in the Darkness: Advent Devotionals from An Intentional Online Community
Based on Year B of the Revised Common Lectionary

Written by the RevGalBlogPal Webring
Edited by Theresa Coleman and Mary Beth Butler
Foreword by Gordon Atkinson, RealLivePreacher.com

A Light Blazes in the Darkness:
Advent Devotionals from An Intentional On line Community.

Copyright © 2005 by Theresa Coleman and Mary Beth Butler, individual contributions copyright held by the authors.

All rights reserved. No portion of this book may be reproduced or transmitted in any form or by any means, electronic or mechanical, including photocopying, recording, or any information storage and retrieval system without the express permission of the editors or the individual authors. For more information email RevGalBlogPals@hotmail.com or email Theresa Coleman at candlemb@bellsouth.net or at 1770 Glen Ryan Court, Loganville, GA 30052. Printed in the USA. Lulu Press, Napa, California, http://www.Lulu.com.

Clipart is royalty free clipart from http://www.clipart.com, a subsidiary of JupiterImages, 5232 E. Pima St., Suite 200C, Tucson, AZ 85712.

Cover design by Streambed Graphics, Grayson Georgia, http://www.streambedgraphics.com.

All proceeds from this book will go to hurricane relief efforts along the US Gulf Coast, hit hard this year by Katrina and Rita.

ISBN 1-4116-5588-5

**For our dear friend and sister,
St. Casserole
http://stcasseroleblog.blogspot.com
who named the need for a group like this one,
and to all those who have also been displaced
by the storms of life this year.**

Foreword

The 17th chapter of John contains the only known prayer offered by Jesus for future generations of his disciples. In this prayer, Christ had only one charge for us. He prayed that we would be one, even as he and the Father are one. Imagine that. Of all the things he could have prayed for, things theological and ecclesiological, Jesus asked for something very simple and childlike. He prayed that his people would be drawn together by what they share in common instead of torn apart by their petty differences.

Sadly, the Church has not been able to live up to the high calling of her Lord. We have not been able to be of one spirit even in local congregations, much less across the diverse and scattered Church universal. Even the lovely differences that we should have celebrated have become fuel for one holy war after another.

Despite this dismal track record, in the season of Advent the frail and sinful children of Christ exchange their swords for wreaths of candles. There is something about this season that turns our thoughts from our differences to what we share in common. Even after all this time, we are still crazy dreamers.

This year, a wonderful group of women ministers from varied denominations, faiths, and traditions, have held hands across the vastness of our geography using the closeness of our technology. They call themselves "The RevGalBlogPal Webring," and their words encompass the full spectrum of human experience. These women of faith are helping us clean the dark glass through which we have looked upon our world. They are pointing to the coming of the light.

Have you longed for peace? Have you searched high and low for moments of grace? Are you afraid that once again you will miss Christmas and see only its frightful, commercial doppelganger that always leaves you feeling empty and unfulfilled? In these pages you will find truth born again in the manger of the commonplace. An Advent pregnancy that brings memories of a past grief, the sudden appearance of an alcoholic at a front door, the battle cry of The Magnificat, the tender memory of a battered strand of bubble lights, the miracle of running water, and the stories of Simeon and Anna, who are surely the patron saints of waiting.

These are songs of spiritual preparation, shared human moments where God's presence became known in the best and the worst of times. Let yourself hope for peace and clarity once again. Look for the light that blazes in the darkness. Take an Advent journey with these pilgrims, who will lead us from Advent, to Christmas, through Epiphany, and even beyond.

Let us join them in our common prayer of Advent.

Come, Lord Jesus.

Gordon Atkinson, www.RealLivePreacher.com
San Antonio, Texas, Fall 2005

Introduction

> *What came into existence was Life, and the Life was Light to live by. The Life-Light blazed out of the darkness; the darkness couldn't put it out.*
>
> **John 1:3-4, The Message**

Once upon a time, on an internet not so very far away, there lived a group of faithful women. The women prayed, laughed, cried and sighed together and soon discovered that they had formed a circle. They were a fellowship, a ring of blogging women – women clergy, women discerning a vocation and their friends, across denominations and countries; an intentional community of unique individuals sharing life together. Over time, the circle widened to include men of faith as well. They had a web-ring, a circle of bloggers, where stories of faith and life could be shared, and friends could be made. They called their circle the RevGalBlogPals and it was and is an intentional community of unique individuals walking together in faith.

It's not a terribly old community. The official birth of the group came from a post by St. Casserole on July 19th of this year, wondering if we could have a t-shirt for the *RevBlogGalPals*. The comments on her posting ran to 114. Within 2 days, reverend mommy had figured out how build a web-ring, reverendmother had designed the first t-shirt and Songbird made a plea for the more inclusive "RevGalBlogPals," which makes room for Blog Pals of Rev Gals who were neither Revs nor Gals. Our ring now circles the globe; we have bloggers from the UK, Canada and Finland, as well as readers from almost every continent.

So this community is no fairy tale, it is real and delightful! You are invited to share in our circle and partake of our fellowship by enjoying *A Light Blazes in the Darkness: Advent Devotionals from an Intentional Online Community*. Be our guests. Make yourselves at home, and feel the blessing of this Advent season as you celebrate it with us. Join us as we wait for the Light to blaze into existence this Advent.

Inner Dorothy, Songbird and reverend mommy

November 27

*Prepare the way, O Zion,
Your Christ is drawing near!
Let every hill and valley
A level way appear.
Greet One who comes in glory,
Foretold in sacred story.
O blest is Christ that came
In God's most holy name.* [1]

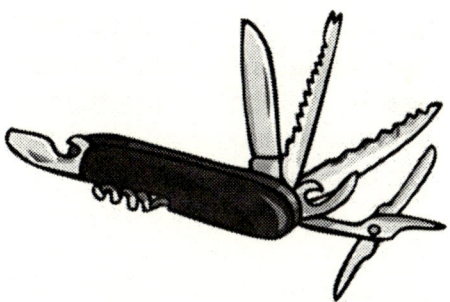

I love my Leatherman© Super Tool. Given to me by a family friend back when I did lots of backpacking and camping, I **know** I walked a little bit lighter and taller when it was attached to my belt. With it, I was prepared for anything and everything. After all, in addition to the standard knife and bottle opener, it comes with multiple screwdrivers, pliers, and wire cutters. Who **doesn't** need multiple ways to cut and strip wires when they are out in the woods?

Prepared is what we are supposed to be. Even now, I want to be prepared for whatever comes my way, whether that means offering prayer in order to calm an anxious heart or having duct tape at the ready.

Being prepared means be ready to handle effectively whatever situation you find yourself in. Handling it so it doesn't take you away from where you want to be and who you want to be while you are there.

Of course, this is exactly the opposite of what it means to prepare for the arrival of Jesus the Christ. Instead of making sure you have the resources to handle whatever comes your way, Advent is about peeling away all of those layers of knowledge and protection that keep you status-quo-bound. Advent is all about allowing yourself to be completely vulnerable so that you can be swept up and away by the Word Made Flesh. Peeling away hurt that protects you from more

---

[1] Text: Adaptation © 1985 Charles P. Price. Used by permission. Inspired by Isaiah 40:3-5 & Luke 3:4-6.

hurt. Peeling away calluses built up from experience, telling you that this year won't be any different. Peeling away the persona you put on to face the world, covering the child God created you to be. What do you need to peel away to reconnect with what is beneath?

The Coming of God is not something we can handle or absorb. It is Impossible! It is exactly the kind of thing that blows us off of our perches and takes us to places that we would never, when we were our former selves, have thought of going. Thanks be to God.

God who arrives in places and times we could never anticipate, thank you. We don't want to handle you; we want to welcome you into our hearts and lives. Show us where to find the courage to abandon those hopes of being ready and help us instead to empty ourselves. May we be filled, when you do arrive, with joy and singing and sharing so fantastic that even the cynics will not be able to resist You. Amen.

Apstraight

November 28

Give ear, O Shepherd of Israel, you who lead Joseph like a flock! You who are enthroned upon the cherubim, shine forth before Ephraim and Benjamin and Manasseh. Stir up your might, and come to save us! Restore us, O God; let your face shine, that we may be saved.

Psalm 80:1-3 (NRSV)

"Christmas is coming, the goose is getting fat; please put a penny in the old man's hat." On Christmas Eve my daughter and her three girl cousins will sing that song at their grandfather's house, just as their dads and mom once did. I can't wait to hear it. It's the season of anticipation. Children feel it particularly. They can't wait for Christmas to come. Even adults have particular things we look forward to in the season. In my small church, we look forward to the annual Hanging of the Greens, and many people tell me how much they treasure the lighting of the candles at the end of the Christmas Eve service. I also look forward to some secular pleasures: seeing the strings of Christmas lights appear around town and especially a large and lively representation of the Grinch on the porch roof of a Victorian house in my neighborhood.

It's against my family traditions to like such things. We never had more than a single, tasteful candle at each window. Why have I come to appreciate the lights so much? I have formed a theory over the past eighteen years, and it is that we need more light here in Maine because it gets so very dark. My hometown in Virginia is just enough further west in the time zone, and enough further south, that sunset comes later than it does for us here. I remember during my first winter in Maine having to turn on the living room lamps at a quarter to three — and that was in a sunny room! It shocked me. Perhaps I hadn't been paying attention before. But I never remember having been so aware of the darkness as I have been living here.

In the Northern Hemisphere, Advent is a time of encroaching darkness. The season of shorter days and longer nights allows us to identify with the people of long ago, those people who knew the rhythms of the year but couldn't explain them scientifically. They had to wonder when the sun would return. They waited, just as we wait for the Son. The waiting is the hardest part. Living with the unknown is like driving after a storm when the streetlights have lost their power; just as we wait and hope for the electricity to return, people of long ago hoped for the light of God to shine again in their lives. The refrain is repeated throughout Psalm 80: *Restore us, O God; let your face shine, that we may be saved.*

In the Psalm the people cry out to God, complaining that their prayers have gone unheeded. They feel abandoned by God. The psalmist names some of the sons of Jacob, the tribes of Israel. They understood themselves to be chosen as God's particular people. Why would God desert them? In that darkness, they could imagine only one source of light: God's face.

There was an Advent when I dwelt in that place of darkness and disconnection.

After losing a baby with a genetic abnormality, I was terrified when I became pregnant again; my history increased the risks for this new pregnancy. I didn't want to tell anyone I was expecting a baby. In both a spiritual and a psychological sense, I was holding my breath until I heard the test results. The short days, and the darkness, both hung on me that year. Where was God in this? The loss of my son two years earlier caused a shift in my understanding of God. I had always been taught that good people were rewarded and bad people suffered, and naïvely I believed it. This meant that quite a few things I didn't like about my life must be my fault, and my usual way of praying was to beg God to change me!

I felt my way through the darkness alone in that Advent of 1994. I needed to find a new way to pray, and it did not come easily. God was not some Santa Claus who would reward my holiness, nor some Grinchy Claus who would take away all that I desired. What was God?

Maybe the problem was not with God, but with me. Just as the Grinch realized Christmas didn't come from a store, I came to understand that God was not as simple as I had imagined. Not unlike the Grinch's undersized heart, my image of God needed to grow three sizes.

But let your hand be upon the one at your right hand, the one whom you made strong for yourself. Then we will never turn back from you; give us life, and we will call on your name. Restore us, O LORD God of hosts; let your face shine, that we may be saved. (Psalm 80:17-19, NRSV)

The psalmist imagined God as a Shepherd whose shining face meant safety to the flock. Whatever happened, whatever the news might be, I could find the strength to face it by keeping my eyes on the Shepherd.

Loving God, we are saved by finding you. Light our way as the days grow shorter. Let your face shine, that we might be saved. Amen.

Songbird

November 29

Grace to you and peace from God our Father and the Lord Jesus Christ. I give thanks to God always for you because of the grace of God which was given you in Christ Jesus, that in every way you were enriched in Him with all speech and all knowledge— even as the testimony to Christ was confirmed among you— so that you are not lacking in any spiritual gift, as you wait for the revealing of our Lord Jesus Christ; who will sustain you to the end, guiltless in the day of our Lord Jesus Christ. God is faithful, by whom you were called into the fellowship of His Son, Jesus Christ, our Lord.

1 Corinthians 1:3-9 (RSV)

This time of year we think much of gifts and giving, but we tend to focus on material rather than spiritual gifts, including memories of gifts given and received from the past.

There were many special dolls and wonderful books that came to me as Christmas gifts. Yet the Christmas memories that are most compelling are those of love and acceptance, both given and received.

I was about five years old the Christmas Eve that a friend of my parents unexpectedly appeared on our doorstep. He and his wife had recently separated. His four year-old daughter was with him for Christmas. He was confused, lost, and bewildered. He didn't know where to go or what to do with his little girl.

There were three of us in the family then— it was before my youngest brother was born. Although my parents had their hands full with 3 kids under the age of 6 hyped up for Christmas, they welcomed these two wanderers and enfolded them into the family.

My father told me many years later how shocked he had been to find that his friend had made no preparations for Christmas Day. Dad didn't want his friend's daughter to watch the rest of us opening our gifts the next morning and have nothing to open herself, so he took his friend to the drugstore, the only place open on Christmas Eve night, to get a few presents for the little girl. This was before the time when stores remained opened late on Christmas Eve for last-minute shoppers.

On another Christmas afternoon many years later, I was reading–probably a book I had received that morning. The house was relatively quiet after the family breakfast and present opening around the tree. Suddenly I heard a woman crying and pounding on our front door. Dad opened the door to a friend who had recently been through a divorce. She and her ex-husband were both alcoholics. She had had too much Christmas "cheer" and now was wallowing in drunken melancholy and regret. All the rest of us scattered. My mother stayed upstairs and didn't come down. We didn't know how to react to this woman whose grief was out of control.

My father, however, greeted her as if she were a much-anticipated guest. He did his best to cheer her up in his own inimitable style. He finally succeeded when he went to his organ (he was an amateur musician) and played loud and fast, getting her to sing Christmas carols with him. By the time she left she was smiling.

"The grace of God that was given you in Christ Jesus, that in every way you were enriched in him with all speech and knowledge…so that you are not lacking in any spiritual gift" wrote Paul to the letter to the Corinthians.

We tend to think of spiritual gifts as the skills of the "church professional:" teaching, preaching, interpretation, prophecy and healing. We forget that often the everyday acts of kindness, charity, and compassion are also spiritual gifts. The gift of hospitality demonstrated by my father in these two situations (and in many others as well) was "revealing of Christ" to his friends and to me.

Thank you, God, for the spiritual gifts You have given us that enrich our lives and testify to the greatest gift of all, Your Son, our Lord Jesus Christ, whose birth we anticipate during this season of Advent. Amen.

Quotidian Grace

November 30

'But in those days, after that suffering,
the sun will be darkened,
and the moon will not give its
light,
and the stars will be falling
from heaven,
and the powers in the heavens
will be shaken.
Then they will see "the Son of Man coming in clouds" with great power and glory. Then he will send out the angels, and gather his elect from the four winds, from the ends of the earth to the ends of heaven.

'From the fig tree learn its lesson: as soon as its branch becomes tender and puts forth its leaves, you know that summer is near. So also, when you see these things taking place, you know that he is near, at the very gates. Truly I tell you, this generation will not pass away until all these things have taken place. Heaven and earth will pass away, but my words will not pass away.

'But about that day or hour no one knows, neither the angels in heaven, nor the Son, but only the Father. Beware, keep alert; for you do not know when the time will come. It is like a man going on a journey, when he leaves home and puts his slaves in charge, each with his work, and commands the doorkeeper to be on the watch. Therefore, keep awake—for you do not know when the master of the house will come, in the evening, or at midnight, or at cockcrow, or at dawn, or else he may find you asleep when he comes suddenly. And what I say to you I say to all: Keep awake.'

Mark 13:24-37 (NRSV)

Just inside the front door of our home hangs a set of sleigh bells. Mind you, these are not the sort of cheesy little jingle bells that are sold everywhere this time of year. No, these are the real McCoy— a matched set of twelve round brass bells, heavy and solid. Once upon a time they were suspended on a leather harness, and served the purpose for which they were created: clearly and cheerfully announcing the progress of horse and wagon or buggy.

But not anymore. For many years they have been tacked in two graduated rows of six onto a polished wooden plaque, placed there by my grandfather's careful hands as a gift for my grandmother. Those bells had been part of her beloved father's legacy to her, one of the familiar sights and sounds of a childhood spent growing up on a farm in central Illinois. Gram had moved off the farm when she married; but she cherished memories from those days all her life, and gladly shared them with me when I'd come over to visit. I loved those stories and would listen for hours, wide blue eyes peeking out from under straight brown bangs as we baked cookies or put up jam or washed dishes. Gram always had things to do at her house.

I could hardly walk past that plaque without touching the bells, and imagining them jangling with the rhythm of a horse trotting along a country road. More than once, Gram let me take them off the wall and give them a shake. "What a racket!" she'd exclaim, smiling. "They really do belong outdoors. You can hear them quite a ways." And then she'd tell a story about hearing those bells as she played in the yard, or helped her mother in the house, or sat in the one-room schoolhouse across the road. She didn't always know what he was doing, or even whether he might be going out or coming home; but the sound meant Pa was nearby.

So now here we are, at the beginning of Advent. In the United States, we've just finished Thanksgiving feasting. We hardly have time to take down the pumpkins and corn stalks before leaping into the excited flurry and bustle that is the usual precursor to Christmas in America. Shopping, and decorating, and baking, and parties, and sending cards and presents...It's as though someone hung out a sign: "Jesus is Coming! Look Busy!!"

Then comes this reading— and it doesn't fit our happy retail imagery at all. Oh, it's about preparation, certainly. But there are no chubby-cheeked cherubs sleeping in tidy mangers with adoring shepherds gathered round, no peaceful snow-covered vistas, and certainly no Jolly Old St. Nicholas. Instead, we have darkened sun and falling stars...and warnings to be ready, to keep awake "for you do not know when the master of the house will come." At first blush, it sounds ominous, almost foreboding.

But is it? Oh, make no mistake, the portrait here is of the Son of Man in all glory, mighty and powerful, as befits the Lord of Life, the Creator of all that is and ever will be. And part of me can't imagine greeting our Savior's return in such a manner without my knees knocking.

But then I remember that this is "the same Lord whose property is always to have mercy," as the old prayer says. The God who made the irrational choice to leave the trappings of omnipotent power behind and to live with us as wholly human, complete with bad hair days and dirt under his fingernails and parents who didn't understand him. The God who loves us enough to call us brother and sister, son and daughter, beloved friend. The God whose very essence is love.

Just as the servants put in charge during the master's absence, we have work to do in the meantime. Good work. "What does the Lord require of you?" the prophet Micah asks. "To do justice, and love mercy, and walk humbly with your God." These are enough to keep us busy in a manner far different than the retail therapy that is our cultural imperative. More challenging, more consuming...more difficult, and infinitely more rewarding.

No, we do not know the day or the hour; but it doesn't matter. We work, and we wait— not in fear and trepidation, but in eager anticipation of the arrival of love.

Like a little girl listening for the sound of Pa's sleigh bells.

Gracious God, help us to see your face in one another, and to so prepare for your coming that we are ready to receive you in joy.

Jane Ellen

December 1

'Not everyone who says to me, "Lord, Lord", will enter the kingdom of heaven, but only one who does the will of my Father in heaven. Everyone then who hears these words of mine and acts on them will be like a wise man who built his house on rock. The rain fell, the floods came, and the winds blew and beat on that house, but it did not fall, because it had been founded on rock. And everyone who hears these words of mine and does not act on them will be like a foolish man who built his house on sand. The rain fell, and the floods came, and the winds blew and beat against that house, and it fell—and great was its fall!'

Matthew 7: 21, 24-27 (NRSV)

Today would have been my mother's 71st birthday. It's my second without her, but I still mark the day with prayer and thanksgiving for all the blessings of her life. My mother was a sensible woman who built her house on rock ... the solid foundation of God's love. Everything my mother did was founded on this love. From the home she created for her family to the inmates she assisted in her job at the county jail. Her days were filled with small acts of kindness to everyone who crossed her path. Sometimes her actions might have seemed a wee bit crazy, but rooted in love she was never really shaken from her overarching desire to share that love.

Mary too must have known the importance of building a house on a solid foundation. I imagine the expectant young mother, readying her life and home for the new child Jesus on the way. This was of course made more complicated by the flight into Egypt and other dramas of the Christmas story. Sometimes her actions might have also seemed a wee bit crazy, like listening to an angel for one thing, but rooted in God's love she was not shaken. Thinking of the teenaged Mary facing the unknown with such faith and trust only increases my awe at the inner strength she must have had. She did not just say, "Lord, Lord," but truly welcomed God into her life ... literally.

It's the first day of December. Only 24 days left to go until Christmas. Many of us I'm sure are overwhelmed by our to do lists and wondering how, in the midst of our busy lives, we will ever manage to get everything done in time.

But what are we busy doing? Are we readying our homes and hearts in expectation of the birth of the child Jesus, or are we instead readying and decorating our houses built on sand? In our culture it is so easy to get wrapped up in the Christmas frenzy. Presents. Shopping. Decorations. Parties. More presents, shopping, decorations and parties. Questions, doubts and general anxiety. Is this the right present? Did I buy enough for my kids? How will I afford it all? Not to mention doubts about the quality of one's own Christmas light display, cookie assortment and holiday hostess prowess. Christmas can sometimes seem like a competition instead of a holy day of prayer and thanksgiving.

A few years ago the Peace & Justice Commission at my parish organized an educational session called "Unplugging the Christmas Machine." The purpose was to help people who felt overwhelmed by Christmas evaluate their plans and decide what was really important in light of the true Christmas message. Unfortunately, many were too busy preparing for Christmas to attend!

I remember one year growing up when my mother was so proud of herself for getting the bulk of her Christmas shopping done ahead of schedule. But she was then faced with a dilemma ... where to hide the presents? The five of us were so adept at finding her hiding places in the house, that given the extra time we would surely discover them and ruin the surprise. She had what she considered a brilliant idea and ended up storing our presents in the trunk of her car, which only she had a key to. Problem solved.

Until one day very close to Christmas she came out of the shopping center to discover the trunk of her car open, and the bulk of the presents stolen. Horror of horrors! Talk about the ultimate Christmas nightmare. What to do? She did not have unlimited funds and had spent most of her Christmas budget on the now stolen presents. For my mother, this was the equivalent of the gale force winds hurling themselves against the house during the storm of the century. Christmas was ruined. No ifs ands or buts about it. Right?

Not really. I remember that Christmas as the best ever. Instead of giving up or spending the rest of the Christmas countdown frantically tracking down each present on her shopping list a second time, my mother decided to simplify things. She purchased the one item each of us really and truly wanted. And she spent the rest of the holiday season at home with her family. Hot Cocoa on a cold winter night. Christmas carols. Stringing popcorn and decorating the tree. Baking cookies. Playing scrabble. Sitting by the fire. Just being together as a family meant more to me than any Cabbage Patch Doll or Barbie RV would have. That Christmas, more than any other, stands out in my memory because it was built on love without all the other things to get in the way.

And when Christmas Eve came and the family went together to midnight mass, it seemed like we were ready to welcome Jesus into our hearts and our home. Which when you get right down to it, is really the whole point of Advent, isn't it?

Loving God, Only 24 days to go until Christmas. Help us to be sensible men and women who spend this time readying to welcome you into our hearts and homes. Do not let us get too distracted by the pressures of the season. Gift us with the wisdom and strength we need to give up our foolish ways. Decorate our hearts with your love. We ask this in Jesus' name. Amen

Susan Rose Francois

December 2

Praise the LORD!
Praise the LORD from the heavens;
praise him in the heights!
Praise him, all his angels;
praise him, all his host!

Praise the LORD from the earth,
you sea monsters and all deeps,
fire and hail, snow and frost,
stormy wind fulfilling his command!

Mountains and all hills,
fruit trees and all cedars!
Wild animals and all cattle,
creeping things and flying birds!

Let them praise the name of the LORD,
for his name alone is exalted;
his glory is above earth and heaven.
He has raised up a horn for his people,
praise for all his faithful,
for the people of Israel who are close to him.
Praise the LORD!

Psalm 148:1-2, 7-10, 13-14 (NRSV)

When I was a child, and probably to this day, my mother kept a box of gifts in the basement of our house. Some of these were small trinkets that could be grabbed for a surprise invitation. Other gifts were picked up throughout the year with specific people in mind for birthdays or for Christmas. I'm not really organized enough to have a box, but I did buy my first Christmas present the other day. It's only September. And, while, I grumble and groan about the holiday paraphernalia lining the shelves before summer is even over, I am beginning to see the value in preparing and planning ahead. Which might explain why I have come to love Advent.

The gift that we receive at Christmas is obvious and glorious – the baby boy born to Mary and Joseph will go on to be the Savior of the world. But the gift that we receive in Advent is a little less flashy, perhaps less dramatic. During the weeks of Advent we are given the opportunity to prepare for the birth of that Savior. These four weeks that we spend draping our spaces in blue provide moments and time for reflection. These are busy weeks, no doubt about it. We rehearse for the pageant and we go caroling and we finish our shopping. We decorate our homes and we serve dinner at the shelter and we address cards to people far away.

Easily enough we forget why we do all of these things and just want the whole thing to be over. When it's January, I think, then I can rest. Psalm 148 calls on all creatures to praise the Lord – earth and sea and sky and all critters that inhabit those places. We go to great lengths to ready ourselves for the glorious birth of Christ, preparing so that we might receive and praise the baby boy. In scurrying about we might grumble and think that it's a whole lot of hoopla for the event of Christmas. However, our hurrying and scurrying is also praising God. We praise the Lord with our whole, in-progress beings.

I love Advent as much for the event that it prepares me for as for the preparation itself.

Writers and painters and artists of all kind talk about the process of creating being just as much art as the finished piece. All of our preparations are just as much praise as the one service of worship and celebration for the birth. We show our love for children not only by welcoming them into the world, but by getting ready for them, too –creating a place in our hearts and homes and lives, a process that takes months, sometimes years.

Advent allows us space for the process of getting ready for Jesus. We sing our praises for God's commanding presence and for the love that God shows to us. During Advent we do what we do to re-order our lives and make a place for Jesus. Clearly we should do this all year–a little bit at a time, constantly reminding ourselves of Jesus' presence in our lives.

And yet, before we make excuses or feel bad and guilty about why we don't always remember Jesus' presence, this season of blue cloths on the altar allows us to start anew. During these four short weeks we reflect on the ways that God has been present with us in the past year—at the birth of a child, at the death of a friend, when the wind and the water whipped too close, in the quiet drive home. We also can pray and hope for the ways that we want God to be present in the coming year—in the rebuilding of a relationship, in the anticipation of a move, in the discernment of a call. We can accept God's presence in our lives for the gift that it is—praising God with all of our being.

During Advent we hear Mary's song and about John the Baptizer, with his wilderness living. With the young girl and the mountain man, we praise God. With the coming of the snow or the warming of the earth, we praise the Lord. With the creatures and the earth, we praise God. With the rest of the world, we prepare for Christmas and praise the Lord.

Lord of All, I give thanks for the chance to prepare for the birth of Jesus. Be with me as I ready my heart and my home, as I reflect on what it means to give praise to you, and as I rejoice that you are always in my life. Amen.

Pink Shoes in the Pulpit

December 3

Since many have undertaken to set down an orderly account of the events that have been fulfilled among us, just as they were handed on to us by those who from the beginning were eyewitnesses and servants of the word, I too decided, after investigating everything carefully from the very first, to write an orderly account for you, most excellent Theophilus, so that you may know the truth concerning the things about which you have been instructed.

Luke 1:1-4 (NRSV)

Lost in the standard Advent readings of the book of Luke is its simple beginning. The gospel account of Luke is, at its heart, an "orderly account" written so that Theophilus may know "the things about which you have been instructed." Luke is a book of stories, of accounts, of things that that were handed on by those who were eyewitnesses and servants of the word.

As we begin our Advent journey–each day progressing closer toward the birth of Christ— we are reminded that this is a special season of beginnings. Luke begins with a preamble, an introduction, a statement of purpose. The writing in this gospel is an orderly account of the events that have been fulfilled among us. But what exactly are those events? And what do they mean to us today?

In beginning our journey toward Christmas, we have an opportunity to reflect upon the events that lead up to Jesus' birth, as well as the events in our own lives that have lead us to newness of life.

Like Theophilus, we have been instructed in the things that make up our faith in Christ. Like him we have been exposed to the truth of the miracle of Christ's birth. But yet, we have a need, deep inside ourselves, to know more; to continue the search for greater knowledge, or perhaps just to understand our faith anew.

It's easy to skip over Luke's preamble and rush into the story of Zachariah and Elizabeth and on into Mary, Joseph and the baby Jesus. But this introduction gives us a moment to pause and to reflect upon the things we know, the things that we think we know and the things that we want to know. How have we experienced Christ in our lives? How has Christ provided us with newness? How can we be servants of the word? What is our own orderly account of how Christ is born in us?

God of newness, provide in us an opportunity to experience your advent today. Begin in us again. Allow us to be open to new ways of your grace. Provide us with new ways of experiencing you this season. May we be awed by you and your love. In Jesus' name we pray. Amen.

Ann

December 4

Comfort, O comfort my people, says your God. Speak tenderly to Jerusalem, and cry to her that she has served her term, that her penalty is paid, that she has received from the Lord's hand double for all her sins.

A voice cries out: 'In the wilderness prepare the way of the LORD, make straight in the desert a highway for our God. Every valley shall be lifted up, and every mountain and hill be made low; the uneven ground shall become level, and the rough places a plain. Then the glory of the LORD shall be revealed, and all people shall see it together, for the mouth of the LORD has spoken."' A voice says, 'Cry out!' And I said, 'What shall I cry?' All people are grass, their constancy is like the flower of the field. The grass withers, the flower fades, when the breath of the LORD blows upon it; surely the people are grass. The grass withers, the flower fades; but the word of our God will stand forever.

Get you up to a high mountain, O Zion, herald of good tidings; lift up your voice with strength, O Jerusalem, herald of good tidings, lift it up, do not fear; say to the cities of Judah, 'Here is your God!' See, the Lord GOD comes with might, and his arm rules for him; his reward is with him, and his recompense before him. He will feed his flock like a shepherd; he will gather the lambs in his arms, and carry them in his bosom, and gently lead the mother sheep.

Isaiah 40:1-11 (NRSV)

I must have been about five years old when my father first took me to a performance of Handel's *Messiah*. I felt unimaginably grown-up as I filed into the local concert hall, and I'm sure my eyes were out on stalks as I watched my first real orchestra tune up and begin the overture. For a while, all was activity, as the strings chased each other in restless counterpoint. Then the mode changed to one of calm expectancy...and it was into this that a tenor dropped his notes of liquid hope '*Comfort ye, Comfort ye my people.*'

A long time has elapsed since that first experience, but it's still almost impossible for me to divorce these words from Handel's inspired music. I think I should, though, because what is going on in this passage is anything but tranquil for much of the time. Of course there is reassurance, that God *will* surely come along the royal road prepared for him, but before he does so there will need to be something very much like an earthquake. Nothing will ever be the same again. Roads aren't built without a dramatic effect on the countryside. Every time a new highway is proposed here, the U.K. press is full of stories of protestors anxious not to see valleys and hills leveled, and the natural landscape altered beyond recognition. No matter that a greater good may be evident— perhaps an historic market town will be freed from the impact of streams of heavy goods vehicles, threatening the foundations of houses that have stood for centuries. Despite this, we're reluctant to opt for change, and this passage speaks of some pretty dramatic changes, including that which makes us most uneasy— our own changed state from earthly life to death. '*The grass withers, the flower fades.*' Now the soundtrack in my head has changed, and I'm carried along by Brahms' *German Requiem,* the drumbeats heavy with anticipation of the inevitable. There will have to be many small deaths as we prepare for the coming of God. The leveling of mountains and hills, the smoothing out of rough places in ourselves and in our community, will never be without cost.

So often Advent becomes a time of frenzied accumulation, as we hunt the length and breadth of town for the perfect gift for people with no material needs whatsoever. Rather than smoothing out valleys and hills, we make mountains out of molehills as the days fly past, until Christmas shopping has become a chore, and we are simply desperate to ensure that there is something, anything, to wrap and put under the tree by December 25th. But the message of Isaiah here reminds us of the transience of all these things, and even of their intended recipients. Instead of accumulation, he speaks of simplification, …and then—oh, then the glory of the Lord will be revealed! What's more, after the images of earthquake and reminders of mortality, the God who comes in might meets us in gentleness. He recognizes the scars that our own inner landscapes bear after so much upheaval, and scoops us up tenderly, as a shepherd a young lamb.

This Advent, many are struggling because their familiar settings have been changed irrevocably, the landmarks of their neighborhood cleared away overnight by the forces of nature. The things they took for granted simply aren't there any more, and like the people of Israel for whom Isaiah wrote, they are refugees, temporary residents in communities that don't feel like home. So these words are for them, too: *'Do not fear...**Here** is your God.'*

Whatever happens to the ephemera around us, that is something we can rely on. May we keep God as the focus as we prepare the way for his coming to each of us at Christmas.

Loving God, in a world whose landscapes are often distorted, help us to clear a pathway for you. Enable us to recognize that your presence with us is all the good news that we need to carry us safely through Advent, and through life, until you welcome us in your loving arms, through Jesus Christ our Savior. Amen.

Kathryn

Amy Avery

December 5

LORD, you were favorable to your land;
you restored the fortunes of Jacob.
You forgave the iniquity of your people;
you pardoned all their sin. Selah
Let me hear what God the LORD will speak,
for he will speak peace to his people,
to his faithful, to those who turn to him in their hearts.
Surely his salvation is at hand for those who fear him,
that his glory may dwell in our land.
Steadfast love and faithfulness will meet;
righteousness and peace will kiss each other.
Faithfulness will spring up from the ground,
and righteousness will look down from the sky.
The LORD will give what is good,
and our land will yield its increase.
Righteousness will go before him,
and will make a path for his steps.
Psalm 85: 1-2, 8-13 (NRSV)

The night was cold and moonlit. The air was crisp and scented with the fragrance of wood smoke from homes alongside the lake. The three of us made our way through the deep snow to our favorite fishing spot of last summer. Our five-year-old daughter and I followed closely in the footsteps of my husband Jim, home for "Christmas in February" again. It seemed as though the Navy always planned these New England celebrations well after the Holiday, but we had our Christmas tree and decorations, and Santa made some special deliveries just for us, including snow we often didn't have in late December. We read again from the gospel of Luke the story of the birth of the One who died to forgive our sins and who came to give us the greatest gift of all.

Blissville Pond in Lisbon, Connecticut was frozen solid. It was a treat for Southerners from Tennessee to watch a pick-up truck fitted with a snowplow drive out onto the ice to clear off a place for skating and ice hockey games. We had never seen lakes freeze so solidly that you could play on them almost all winter long. You could probably walk across the lake to visit neighbors in those houses with the glowing windows and warm fireplaces. The snow was deep and coated with a thin, crunchy cover of ice. Our footsteps almost echoed as we made our way down the slope to the spot where last year we had caught those plump little sunfish and bass. Daddy had been at sea in a submarine that past summer, but we had made sure to take pictures of mother and daughter smiling and holding up the "big fish" for the camera. Now, it was hard to believe anything could survive under the shining surface of a foot or two of ice.

No need for "Mr. Reg" and his snowplow tonight. The ice was perfect across the six-acre lake. Not a wrinkle or a ripple appeared on that smooth surface. We huddled together for warmth and stood amazed at the beauty of God's creation. Crystalline bits of frost drifted down from the branches and the little trailer park where we lived was transformed into our own special winter wonderland. We didn't have much in the way of material possessions back then, but we had our faith and each other, and we had love.

The Psalmist tells us that love, faithfulness, righteousness and peace will meet each other just as the star-filled night sky met the snow and ice that winter's night. Faithfulness will spring up from the ground as the grass and wildflowers would spring up to replace the path we left on the snow-covered embankment. Righteousness will look down from heaven as sure as the rain falls and as certainly as we expect God's love to yield crops of goodwill and peace.

To our daughter, the snow covering our familiar route was an obstacle she didn't understand. Wearing her snowsuit and boots, she thought it would be easy after leaving the cleared road to make her way by walking beside daddy. She would walk a few steps on top of the snow, and then she'd sink nearly to her waist in a drift. She learned that with comforting hands holding hers and a trail already blazed, her route was made easy. So we can remember the loving hands of our Heavenly Father who holds onto our own and provides a path for our steps through the sacrifice of His Son. Do we remember to try to place our feet in the steps of the path He walked for us? Pathways of life become so much easier if we stick to the road he paved with his Word.

I don't know which of us first did the same familiar thing we always used to do in the summer. One of us picked up a nice, small flat stone and casually leaned down with a sidearm flick of the wrist and skipped the stone as though it might hop or jump several times and then plop into warm summer water. It skimmed the mirrored surface without a bounce or a bump. On and on it traveled, making an eerie sound that none of us had ever heard before. The extreme quiet and stillness of the winter night permitted a strange noise to resound along with the stone out onto the pond. The stone went further than any pebble had ever traveled over the surface of the unfrozen lake in the summer. We began to dig in the snow of the lakeshore to find more and more of the little rocks with a nice flat surface. It was an amazing night as we continued to toss those flat stones across the pond beyond our wildest expectations. We think that some of them even traveled the entire distance between our shore and the closest houses on the far side. We could hear them as they sang along the ice, the most unusual sound we had ever heard. It seemed a reminder of eternity.

    Snow began to fall and the time of "singing" stones across the lake ended with us retracing our path home. The following morning the lake had a fresh layer of snow over the ice and no stone would be skipping across to the other side. We have tried it again and again over the years at many different places, but never have the right combination of circumstances existed that resulted in the same effect of sound, sight or distance. The stones singing across the pond that icy night resound in my ears nearly thirty years later.

    I remember those Christmas celebrations we had when we waited long past other Decembers, but I remember this one most of all. I have known people in my life that seemed like those stones, skimming along a straight way until their love and faithfulness met the sky and their souls sailed on into eternity with Him. It is a good memory and one in which we can see the pathways of our lives and of the path we will tread if we follow in the footsteps of our Lord.

Gentle and Loving Creator, we listen to the words of love and joy that you speak to our souls. We look to You for guidance on the unfamiliar roads of our lives and sing out with love for You. May we travel on this earth with our hands in Yours and be guided into eternal life through the grace of your Son, Jesus Christ. Amen.

Auntie Em

December 6

My soul magnifies the Lord,
and my spirit rejoices in God my Savior...
God has shown strength with God's arm,
and has scattered the proud in the thoughts of their hearts.
God has brought down the powerful from their thrones,
and lifted up the lowly;
God has filled the hungry with good things,
and sent the rich away empty.

Luke 1:46-47, 51-53 (NRSV)

This is a portion of the song Mary sings during her pregnancy with Jesus. It is an improvisation of the song Hannah sang after the birth of her son Samuel. The words have been set to music countless times, but my favorite setting is John Rutter's *Magnificat*. The year that I found my way back to Christ, as a young adult, our church choir presented that glorious work in worship, and the rehearsals were a deep spiritual discipline for me. The soaring, joyful melodies provided the ideal soundtrack to that homecoming, to that first Christmas season back in the church.

It was only years later, when I was able to read Mary's Magnificat without Rutter's festive score ringing through my head, that I fully realized: the Magnificat is not a sweet lullaby.

It is a battle cry, bold and defiant.

Mary sings for the weak and the lowly, the poor and the hungry. Every hurting son is now her son; every hungry daughter is now her daughter. Before, they were simply among her; now, they dwell within her. And the song erupts from that place deep down where she carries them, where she bears them in her own body.

It is not necessary to be a mother, or even a parent, to feel such empathy. But one of the gifts and curses of pregnancy and motherhood for me is that I sometimes experience the pain of the weak and the lowly and the hungry and the hurting on a physical level. A cellular level. I never did before.

Something terrible happened recently to the loved one of a loved one, a beautiful and brave young woman. I dare not say what; the story is not mine to tell. The details are unimportant anyway, because it's a story of violence that's repeated daily around the world, a story that many beloved women in my life share. I will not tell their tales, but I can sing a song for them. And the song that I sing asks, begs, *demands* that God be strong in the gathering and the filling and the lifting up.

The day I found out about this terrible thing in the life of my young friend, my husband and I had tickets that night to see the Indigo Girls in concert. I carried this young woman's story, and the stories of countless others, as I went.

Those of you familiar with the folk duo probably know that die-hard fans usually have a "favorite" Indigo Girl. As for me, I have always preferred Emily Saliers's songs to Amy Ray's. Emily's seem more interesting musically, more delicately textured. Her lyrics operate on many levels and are especially ripe with biblical images. Amy's songs are more straightforward. They are linear, direct, sharp like an arrow. Both women write powerful songs. Emily's songs are powerful in their beautiful complexity; Amy's, in their defiance.

So Emily is my favorite, but that night, Amy was singing to and for the women whose stories I carried in my body, whose pain I felt. Amy sings the Magnificat the way it is meant to be sung—thunderous, proud, piercing the soul.

> "I saw a woman on the sidewalk…
> she was beaten by a stranger.
> (Danger Danger Danger Danger)."[2]

Amy holds the audience rapt. She is singing their song.

> "Let it ring
> in the name of the man that set you free
> Let it ring
> And the strife will make me stronger
> As my maker leads me onward
> I'll be marching in that number
> So let it ring
> One day we'll all be free
> Let it ring."[3]

---

[2] Ray, Amy. "Chickenman." *Rites of Passage*. CD.
[3] Ray, Amy. "Let It Ring." *Prom*. CD.

Our secular culture's way of doing Christmas clatters noisily against the church's quiet observance of Advent. While radio stations play cheerful holiday tunes 24/7, we dare to sing, "O Come O Come Emmanuel." Why do we bid the savior to come? Not to create some false dramatic buildup to December 25 (will the baby arrive again this year? of course he will, and right on time too). No, we bid the savior to come because we still need a savior. The world still needs healing and hope. The stories of hurt, violence and oppression that we carry within us remind us of this reality. And so, we sing. Defiantly, expectantly, confident in the God who shows strength and mercy, in hope for the day when all will be free, we sing.

We sing to you, O God, and to the Savior for whom we wait.
Come quickly, Lord Jesus.
Come for the sake of a wounded world.
Amen.

Reverend Mother

December 7

*The beginning of the good news of Jesus Christ, the Son of God.
As it is written in the prophet Isaiah,
'See, I am sending my messenger ahead of you,
who will prepare your way;
the voice of one crying out in the wilderness:
"Prepare the way of the Lord,
make his paths straight,"'*

John the baptizer appeared in the wilderness, proclaiming a baptism of repentance for the forgiveness of sins. And people from the whole Judean countryside and all the people of Jerusalem were going out to him, and were baptized by him in the river Jordan, confessing their sins. Now John was clothed with camel's hair, with a leather belt around his waist, and he ate locusts and wild honey. He proclaimed, 'The one who is more powerful than I is coming after me; I am not worthy to stoop down and untie the thong of his sandals. I have baptized you with water; but he will baptize you with the Holy Spirit.'

Mark 1: 1-8 (NRSV)

We Christians have our own December dilemma. Where our Jewish, Muslim or Hindu neighbors may struggle to maintain their religious identities in the midst of the Christmas barrage, we struggle to maintain our spiritual integrity in the midst of a festival, which still bears the name of our Savior, but has become largely a secular extravaganza. The "Holiday Events" insert in our local paper last year had a separate category for "Religious Christmas Events." All righty then!

Some of us place a total ban on Santa, elves, Rudolph, Frosty, and Chestnuts Roasting on an Open Fire. Most of us, though, spend the season walking the tightrope stretched carefully between the Advent Wreath and the Christmas Tree. We don't want to be dour old Puritans, but we don't want to forget the Reason for the Season either.

Last December, a house I passed on the drive to my kids' school displayed a banner exhorting, ***Keep Christ in Christmas***! This is a brave proclamation in unchurched Oregon. But as I considered the tensions of the season, I wondered if perhaps I should whip up a few banners proclaiming, ***Keep John the Baptist in Advent!***

We tend to assume that the big boxing match of the season pits Santa in the ring against Jesus. I'm not so sure. Maybe the real action is the competition between Santa and John the Baptist.

Consider:

- Santa and John the Baptist are both big guys with wild hair and weird outfits— red fur or camel's hair: take your pick.
- Santa and John the Baptist both have odd dietary requirements: milk and cookies or locusts and honey.
- Santa and John the Baptist both reside in hostile wilderness environments: the North Pole and the Judean desert, respectively.
- Santa and John the Baptist both proclaim a word of judgment and a word of promise. Here the similarities end.

Santa's word of judgment consists of "making a list and checking it twice." The naughty are cast into the outer darkness of toy deprivation. Santa's promise, on the other hand, is that those deemed "nice" will be rewarded with the fulfillment of their every consumeristic desire. So you better not pout, you better not cry.

John's word of judgment would singe Santa's eyebrows. *We're all naughty!* Every last breathing one of us. There is no bargaining. There is no last minute full court press of good behavior that can save us. The only cure for what ails us is repentance for our sins in the hope of God's forgiveness. John's promise is that there is One coming that is greater than he— One who can fulfill the deepest desires of our souls through the power of the Holy Spirit.

Mark reports that lines formed in the desert from all the people who flocked to hear John's preaching and be baptized.

One holiday season I made a rare trip to the mall, kids in tow, hoping to complete my Christmas shopping in a one afternoon blitz of grim determination. (Did I mention that I'm not fond of shopping unless it involves a bookstore?) As we dashed from Made in Oregon to Nordstrom's, my small daughter gasped with delight. She had caught sight of Santa's Village and the long line of children waiting for their turn on Santa's lap.

"Please Mom! Please!" she pleaded.

What to do? The pastor in me wants to limit any child's exposure to the cult of Santa. The parent in me worries that my children will be scarred for life if I do not let them participate in this great American childhood ritual. We joined the line.

Ever the multi-tasker, I used the wait time to muse upon my not-yet-finished sermon on John the Baptist. How easy it is, I reflected, to join the wrong line. The world pushes us toward the line at the end of which we whisper our fantasies to a jolly fulfiller of wishes. The gospel calls us to join the line at the end of which we confess our sins, enter the waters of forgiveness, and look to the One who is to come.

You better not shout, you better not cry.
Better not pout, I'm tellin' you why.
Santa Claus is coming to town.

On Jordan's banks the Baptist's cry
Announces that the Lord is nigh.
Awake and hearken, for he brings
Glad Tidings of the King of kings.

Dear Lord, guide us into the right lines where we wait for the right things. Help us long for what lies beyond our wishes and hope for One who is greater than any we have met thus far. Amen

Rebel Without a Pew

December 8

But do not ignore this one fact, beloved, that with the Lord one day is like a thousand years, and a thousand years are like one day. The Lord is not slow about his promise, as some think of slowness, but is patient with you, not wanting any to perish, but all to come to repentance. But the day of the Lord will come like a thief, and then the heavens will pass away with a loud noise, and the elements will be dissolved with fire, and the earth and everything that is done on it will be disclosed. Since all these things are to be dissolved in this way, what sort of persons ought you to be in leading lives of holiness and godliness, waiting for and hastening the coming of the day of God, because of which the heavens will be set ablaze and dissolved, and the elements will melt with fire? But, in accordance with his promise, we wait for new heavens and a new earth, where righteousness is at home. Therefore, beloved, while you are waiting for these things, strive to be found by him at peace, without spot or blemish; and regard the patience of our Lord as salvation.

2 Peter 3:8-15 (NRSV)

So much of Scripture is filled with the anticipation of the day of the Lord arriving in sound and fury, loud noises and fire. Our Advent readings are filled with it. And yet, what is Advent about? It's about waiting for a baby. And when we think of the baby in the standard Nativity scene, it seems peaceful. We see Mary cradling her child, with Joseph standing nearby. We see the shepherds arriving in quiet awe. Reconciling our moments at the crèche with Advent passages like this from 2 Peter can give us a collective headache.

But babies arrive in sound and fury. The delivery of new life is marked by the pain of the mother in labor and the cries of the child as it leaves the womb.

We can see all the signs of the advent of a baby, but in the end, a baby arrives when it's ready. Not at the choice of the parents, not by the wish of the doctor. The family is in the baby's hands.

At the same time, one knows a baby is on the way. There are things to be done, nurseries to prepare, diapers to buy. Even the most frugal of families has to change its habits and its home for a baby. The deadline of new life sharpens the urgency of all of these tasks. Because the arrival of the baby will reveal all the shortcomings of the family it is arriving into. Any untended emotional issues, any flaws in how the family functions together, will be laid bare in the days and years to come.

And yet, with all the pressure and work to do, it is a joyful time. New life is being created. A new family is on the way.

Humans tend to read passages about apocalypses with fear. The Lord is coming in judgment. Better clean up your act so you'll measure up! You don't want to receive the divine equivalent of coal in your stocking on Christmas morning, do you?

Instead of being afraid, or living in a pinched version of morality, what if we found this time to be one of urgent and joyful expectation of the new life to come? Of the new family in Christ that is being created?

No family is perfect. No one of us will be perfect when the day of the Lord comes. What family is perfectly prepared for its new arrival, for all the ways in which one baby is going to turn lives upside down.

This baby we're waiting for turned the whole world upside down.

It's the second week of Advent and there's still time to clear a little room in the home of our souls as a nursery for the Christ child. There's still time to imagine the changes that are coming. There's still time to think about some new habits—of prayer, of giving, of letting go of self as the center of the universe. God is giving us extra time because the ultimate divine goal is salvation of all.

Perfection in righteousness isn't possible in this lifetime, but every inch of room we convert in our hearts gives us a glimpse of the new life in the family God is making for us.

Lord of hopefulness and joy, we give you thanks for the patience you have for the whole human race, and for this Advent time of preparation for your coming. Deliver us from the tyranny of habits which control us and block us from you, and give us strength to pursue those which draw us nearer to your presence. We ask this in the name of the Christ who came into the world as a baby, to make us a new family in You. Amen.

Emily at Hazelnut Reflections

December 9

When you search for me, you will find me; if you seek me with all your heart, I will let you find me, says the LORD.
Jeremiah 29:13-14a (NRSV)

When I first met my friend G, he was rehearsing for a performance of the Mendelssohn oratorio *Elijah*, which contains a tenor aria taken from this Scripture. "If with all your hearts ye truly seek..." he sang. G and I became friends because at the time I knew him he didn't have a car, and we had some destinations in common, so I became one of his "carpool friends." In fact, one of my happiest memories of G is a memory of an Advent evening when we were driving in a heavy, silent snow—huge, fat flakes drifting down slowly, white against the dark of evergreens and the orange of street lights, glistening on the ground—and we were singing snatches of Handel's *Messiah* to one another, enjoying ourselves, as if time would last forever. Our friendship was not always easy. We argued and forgave, disappointed one another and gave to one another, found ourselves distant at times and closer at others. I began to feel that G's place in my heart was a 'family place,' that he was, on some spiritual level, a brother of mine. I don't know what he thought—that depended from day to day. G was a restless spirit, who had tried a million things in life and had a million plans.

G became ill and was diagnosed with full-blown AIDS. This was years ago; before the drugs existed that now offer at least some people hope for years of reasonable-quality life. His condition progressed rapidly, and I was one of a huge raft of people who took part in attempting to care for him. Together the group of us shopped for groceries, did laundry, interpreted medical results, took G out for social occasions, cleaned his house, listened late at night when he was alone and afraid, and tried with varying degrees of success to cope with G's need for independence. The loss of agency was a loss G mourned bitterly in his illness, and there were times when despite my desire to be of helped I stepped exactly wrong and hurt his feelings instead. So we still struggled; we still loved and hurt and disappointed and forgave. And he was still my brother.

All G's relationships in those last months were a dance of closeness followed by lashing out, but it is a measure of the greatness of his heart that, on the day he died, a group of us gathered at his bed, and each of us was a person who had been "fired" by G in at least one role, at least once. Still, we were there, as he knew at some level we would be, to love him through this great transition. When I arrived (we were skidding from all over town across ice-covered intersections on a winter morning) our friend W, himself a gifted musician, was singing softly to G, singing the same aria that had begun our friendship: "If, with all your hearts, ye truly seek…" W said what has stuck in my mind ever since: that, at the end, this promise of faith is one worth hearing.

There was a memorial service for G, and another of his musician friends sang. A glorious contralto, she picked for her contribution…that exact aria! And I sat, and wept, at the words and the promise. When I told her afterward of the multilayered connections between G, W, me, beginning, end, and those words, she was stunned. She had had no idea. She just felt it right to sing that particular piece. We stood and had goose bumps together, G's last gift to either of us. He always liked surprises. And he loved having the last word.

From that day forward this Scripture has been a solid rock at the core of my faith. It speaks to a God of passionate involvement, a God whose promise is unflagging, a God who will not hide from the wholehearted seeker, a God who does not require specific words or specific rituals, a God who requires simply nothing more or less than our whole hearts. That same God who called to Mary and called to

Joseph, that same God who calls to us each and every waiting day of Advent, *promises* that as long as we seek with our hearts we shall find. No doubts and no exceptions.

Almighty and amazing God, we thank You for the promise to reveal Yourself, if we seek You with all our hearts. Help us to lean on that promise when we feel far away from You. Help us to lean on that promise when our churches are less than helpful in our seeking. Help us to lean on that promise when the waiting seems too long and hard. And help us to seek You in Advent season, so that, as your Son was born into the world, You will burst also into our hearts and souls and lives. Amen.

Terri Colburn

December 10

"For thus says the Lord of hosts: Once again, in a little while, I will shake the heavens and the earth and the sea and the dry land; and I will shake all the nations, so that the treasure of all nations shall come, and I will fill this house with splendor, says the Lord of hosts. The silver is mine and the gold is mine, says the Lord of hosts. The latter splendor of this house shall be greater than the former, says the Lord of hosts; and in this place I will give peace, says the Lord of hosts."

Haggai 2:6-9 (NRSV)

*Silver and gold, silver and gold,
ev'ryone wishes for silver and gold.
How do you measure its worth?
Just by the pleasure it gives here on earth.*

*Silver and gold, silver and gold,
mean so much more when I see
Silver and gold decorations
on ev'ry Christmas tree.*[4]

As shining ornaments adorn homes and line retail aisles, our minds often turn to presents and decorations long before Christmas actually comes. Silver and gold become color schemes and descriptions of costly gifts. As the Christmas carol says, "Ev'ryone wishes for silver and gold," for the pleasure they bring here on earth, for the beauty they lend to people, buildings, and yes, Christmas trees.

It seems almost trite to critique our obsession with the material side of Christmas; after all, every sensible Christian I know has already done so. However, it's always interesting to me to see how quickly we tend to jump into the celebration of Christmas. As the stores stock lights, ornaments, and gifts earlier every year, we likewise

---

[4] Words and Music by Johnny Marks

begin to decorate and rejoice before even Advent has begun – a bit prematurely to my mind. We forget that there is an aspect of *waiting* implicit in this period of time before the big celebration. We forget that we're not there yet.

We're not the first people to have this problem; Haggai's audience also suffered from a touch of premature celebration syndrome. In 538 B.C., the Jews had been allowed to return to Jerusalem to begin rebuilding the temple that had been destroyed by the Babylonians. After two years, they completed the foundation and began a time of great rejoicing. Neighboring nations, threatened by their success, managed to halt the building of the temple for several years. However, even when a new king supported the rebuilding of the temple, the Jews did not move forward. The prophet Haggai, therefore, spoke to a group of people reveling in a temple that was not yet even halfway completed.

"The silver is mine and the gold is mine, declares the Lord of hosts." Probably a reference to the splendor of the first temple, God reminds the Jews – and us – that all of those things humans use to give pleasure and beauty do not in fact belong to us; they belong to God. The unfinished temple belongs to God, as does its glorious completion.

"The latter splendor of this house shall be greater than the former, says the Lord of hosts; and in this place I will give peace, says the Lord of hosts." The other important reminder here is that God's work is not yet complete; they're not there yet. It's fine to be glad about the things they already have, but God is in the process of doing something bigger and better, of making a house even greater than Solomon's temple, and of granting *peace*.

One part of Advent for us is waiting for something that has already come; although in the Church year we wait to celebrate Christmas, the birth of Jesus Christ has in fact already happened. God has in that sense already fulfilled the promise to "shake all nations." The birth of Jesus shook the core of this world, and we are right to rejoice in his coming.

And yet, we are still a people in waiting. We wait for all nations to come together and fill God's house with glory. We wait for the "latter splendor of this house" to be complete. We wait for God's peace to be delivered.

Advent is the time in which we recognize that we're not there yet, that God is doing something bigger and better in this world. We realize that it's good to be joyful for what we have already received, but we also remember that God has promised that there is more to come.

So, during the season of Advent, we enjoy the parties, the decorations, the presents. We worship with the increasing light symbolized by the candles of our Advent wreath. We prepare ourselves to celebrate the birth of our Lord. And we wait for a time that has been promised, a time when all nations will gather together in the glory of God's completed house, a time when there will truly be peace on earth.

Lord of hosts, the silver is yours and the gold is yours, as are all things. Grant us your presence and your peace as we wait for the time in which all nations will gather and your glory will be complete, and as we hope for the fulfillment of all your promises to bring this earth your peace. Amen.

Rev. Stacey

December 11

The Spirit of the Sovereign LORD is on me,
  because the LORD has anointed me
to preach good news to the poor.
He has sent me to bind up the brokenhearted,
to proclaim freedom for the captives
and release from darkness for the prisoners,
'For I, the LORD, love justice; I hate robbery and iniquity. In my faithfulness I will reward them and make an everlasting covenant with them. Their descendants will be known among the nations and their offspring among the peoples. All who see them will acknowledge that they are a people the LORD has blessed.' I delight greatly in the LORD; my soul rejoices in my God. For he has clothed me with garments of salvation and arrayed me in a robe of righteousness, as a bridegroom adorns his head like a priest, and as a bride adorns herself with her jewels. For as the soil makes the sprout come up and a garden causes seeds to grow, so the Sovereign LORD will make righteousness and praise spring up before all nations.

Isaiah 61:1, 8-11 (NIV)

An emaciated toddler, gasping in extremis, lies on the ground in a drought-parched African village as a vulture patiently waits just yards away.

A sobbing prisoner of war braces for the bullet that is about to explode into his skull, point blank, at the hands of his captor.

A rescuer reaches for a drowning woman, clutches her outstretched hand– but then the flood current pulls them apart; we see his anguish and her terror, their arms still reaching for one another across the roiling water.

Last year I visited an exhibition of Pulitzer Prize winning photographs. These are some of the images from that exhibition– captured moments of particular places and times that nonetheless speak to the timelessness and universality of suffering in this world— that will be seared into my consciousness forever. They broke my heart. I like to think of myself as a mentally tough person, but I found myself sitting on a bench in the hallway with my stinging eyes closed, choking back sobs.

> *O God, make speed to save us*
> *O Lord, make haste to help us.*

How often have those words, those thoughts, ascended to the heavens over the centuries? *Help us. Save us.* How many "pictures in an exhibition" does each of us keep in the dark hallways of our memory – mental snapshots of scenes from collective horrors like 9/11 or the aftermath of Hurricanes Katrina and Rita, or more personal portraits of pain engraved in our minds, pictures that only we can see?

The lesson for today, from the Book of Isaiah, is a proclamation that *help is on the way.*

Sometimes it's so hard for us to believe that help is on the way. And that was true for the original readers and hearers of this passage as well. They were returnees— Jews who, after being forced into exile in a foreign land, were finally able to go home again. But when they returned home they found the reality of life there to be something far less than the idealized prophetic visions of a restored Jerusalem that had fueled their hope during the exile. Raised expectations followed by disillusionment— how often does this cycle play itself out in human history? Exiles of other lands return home to greet hardship and disappointment. Hopeful immigrants arrive to find that the streets of their new country aren't paved with gold after all. And think of our own personal histories of "dreams deferred"— life stories that have departed from the scripts we counted on.

And— dare it be said?— sometimes, especially in this season of heightened expectations, when we are constantly bombarded with images of greeting-card-perfect holidays that our own experience can never match, and studiously cheery messages promising peace and goodwill even as the 24-hour news channels flash image upon image of more global mayhem and suffering, we can lose faith in The Story itself.

Help us. Save us.

The Servant of Isaiah 61 reaches one hand back to his dispirited people and one hand into the future, all the way to us. His cruciform grasp pulls us all toward him. *Come here*, he says. *I want to show you something.* And he does. The brokenhearted healed. The imprisoned set free. The faint of heart given courage. The lowliest, most disempowered, given honor and dignity. New images— images that each of us frame in our own cultural and personal ways; word-pictures that kindle the tiniest flickers of light in the dim embers of our hearts.

    Sometimes we need to be reminded of The Story— that God's saving action in history is leading to a time when, in the words of medieval mystic Julian of Norwich, all will be well and all will be well and all manner of thing will be well. The author of Isaiah 61 knew that we need to be reminded, as he penned his majestic images of wrongs made right and broken places mended. These images are an invitation to continue to walk in God's gallery of hope, gaining strength from the visions of the future that have been given to us— and not only these, but the images of the inbreaking Reign of God that we can see around us with the eyes of faith: a life saved from chaos and nihilism by an encounter with the Divine and the embrace of caring others; a family caught in a natural disaster, being literally snatched out of the death and destruction around them and given a new start in a new community; a prisoner of conscience released from captivity after steady international pressure from persons of goodwill; despotic governments finally crumbling in the wake of citizens seeking freedom. Each picture of God's saving power gives us the strength to make our way to the next, knowing that at the end of this exhibition we will find not a final, valedictory image, but God — the God Who Saves Us— face-to-face, at long last, reaching for us once more: *Come here. I want to show you something.*

God of our salvation: It is so easy for us to lose heart in this world. Sometimes we lose sight of who you are; sometimes we cannot see your saving action in the world and in our lives. Thank you for the witness of your prophets, who help us remember that you hold history in your hand and us in your heart, and who have pointed the way toward the coming of our Savior. Help us hold on to the promise that you are with us always, and that we will be yours forever. Help us proclaim, both by what we say and by what we do, the good news of your deliverance. Help us live your shalom into the world wherever and whenever and however we can. We pray these things in the name of our Lord Jesus Christ. Amen.

Lutheranchik

December 12th

*When the Lord restored the fortunes of Zion
we were like those who dream.
Then our mouth was filled with laughter,
and our tongue with shouts of joy;
then it was said among the nations,
'The Lord has done great things for them.'
The Lord has done great things for us,
and we rejoiced.
Restore our fortunes, O Lord,
like the watercourses of the Negeb.
May those who sow in tears
reap with shouts of joy.
Those who go out weeping,
bearing the seeds for sowing,
shall come home with shouts of joy,
carrying their sheaves.*

Psalm 126 (NRSV)

Joy. Pure, adulterated, unexpected, unearned joy. The Psalmist longs for it, and as children of God, so do we. Remember the feeling of being caught off guard by joy?

I'm not talking about just plain old happiness. Happiness is something that if we think about it long enough, we can squash like a bug. I can usually think of ten reasons at any given moment to not be happy. But joy sneaks up on you when you least expect it; joy *owns* you, often in a way you don't anticipate.

Recently we had a strange and wonderful week in my family. Tuesday was the strangest of all. It started out with a driving rain. But before Tuesday even got here, the well-oiled machine I call our family's life had blown a gasket—literally. The car my son drives had broken down on a major street very early Sunday morning, and that threw the whole family system into crisis mode; everyone in my family had commitments, and well, the whole thing just works out better if there is the same number of cars as people who have to drive places. So by Tuesday morning, we were operating on "Plan B".

Plan B involved a rental car, and that's what my spouse and son were taking care of on that rainy Tuesday morning. But my son was running late to school, and I was breaking my cardinal rule of not driving and using the cell phone at the same time, because the high school had to be called and explanations had to be made. And the rain kept pouring down. My spouse called and told me that the rental car place had made a rather unusual decision regarding what car they rented to him. But in the meantime, I had meetings.

I made my morning meeting, and I got to the church and did what I needed to do, and I drove to my three-hour afternoon/evening meeting, and by the time I got home, I was beat, and really tired of driving in the rain. I was in my pajamas, getting really settled in for the night when my spouse came home from his evening commitment and said, "Come out to the driveway."

Oh, yes, the rental car! The rain had finally stopped, so I threw on my slippers and a sweatshirt, and walked out...and there it was: my dream car. A Jaguar X-Type. I've never actually touched one, but I reached out and petted the hood ornament, "Nice kitty," I purred. "You want to drive it?" "Are you crazy?" I grabbed the key and got in.

I didn't leave the subdivision, and I was only behind the wheel of that car for about five minutes, but I think my spouse will confirm this: I was beyond words for those five minutes. I don't like to think of myself as a particularly materialistic person, and I resolved myself a long time ago to the fact that I will never own a car like the one I drove Tuesday night, and I would have to say that I am generally okay with that. My dream car was always something that I could admire from afar, but something that I was okay having not experienced first hand. But now I have, and I can say it was as wonderful as I expected. And no matter when the car goes back to the rental office, no matter how long I live, I drove one for five minutes, and nothing can change that. Nobody can take that away from me.

So...if I'm not materialistic, and I'm happy driving my Hyundai around, where did that joy that left me speechless and making this sound, (unintelligible, guttural exhale) come from?

I think it comes from this: We are not Jaguar people. We are Hyundai people, we are 10-year-old minivan people, we are broken down Ford Taurus in the auto repair shop people. And we like it that way. (Except for the auto repair part!) That's what we are accustomed to. So when a Jaguar comes into our life, one we didn't expect, one in fact we thought we'd never get to actually see up close, we assume the rental place made a huge mistake. It's not what we asked for. It's not even what we dreamed of. It's not the agreement that was made between the rental agent and us. It's luxury sports car at subcompact prices. We might be nervous about it being in the driveway; nervous about what the neighbors might think. But not nervous enough to kill the joy.

The Psalmist is singing of restorative joy. For those of us who spend our days sowing seeds of disillusionment and disappointment, Gods' plan for us includes joy that life circumstances cannot take away, a deliverance from weeping, a restoration to the joy God wants each of us to experience. Thanks be to God!

Gracious and loving God, into the ordinariness of our lives, you bring us joy beyond our wildest dreams. Help us to be on the lookout for you in every aspect of our lives. When our deliverance comes, let us acknowledge that all good comes from you. May we bring the best of what we are in service for you. In Christ's name, Amen.

Revmom/Cheesehead

December 13

Be joyful always; pray continually; give thanks in all circumstances, for this is God's will for you in Christ Jesus. Do not put out the Spirit's fire; do not treat prophecies with contempt. Test everything. Hold on to the good. Avoid every kind of evil. May God himself, the God of peace, sanctify you through and through. May your whole spirit, soul and body be kept blameless at the coming of our Lord Jesus Christ. The one who calls you is faithful and he will do it.

1 Thessalonians 5:16-24 (NIV)

Today the feast of Saint Lucia (also known as Saint Lucy) is celebrated in Nordic countries. Early on the morning of December 13, the oldest daughter in the family rises and wakes each of her family members. She is dressed in a long, white gown with a wide red sash and wears a crown made of a wreath with nine lit candles. Saint Lucia was a young woman who was martyred for her faith. She lived in fourth century Syracuse during a time of terrible persecution of Christians. Much of the story has been lost over the years but according to one, Lucia's eyes were put out while she was tortured for her Christian beliefs. Another story says she may have plucked her own eyes out to protest the persecutions of the Christians. In Finland, Sweden, Norway, Denmark and Iceland the feast of Saint Lucia marks the beginning of the Christmas season.

Her name is derived from the Latin word *lux* which means light, and I believe that it is no coincidence that her feast is celebrated here in the north during the darkest time of the year. In some places there is no daylight at all for most of Advent, and even for those of us who live in the more southerly parts of Scandinavia, the sun only briefly raises its head before sinking sadly into the grey sky only a few hours later.

Light is very important to all of us: physiologically and mentally, but also spiritually. Jesus said of Himself: "I have come into the **world** as a **light**, so that no one who believes in me should stay in darkness." (John 12:46) We know that where there is no light there is only darkness, but where there is even a chink of light, the darkness has to recede. This fact reassures me a lot!

Today's scripture encourages us to "be joyful always, pray continuously and give thanks in all circumstances for this is God's will for you in Christ Jesus" (1 Thessalonians 5:16-18). We can and should be joyful and thankful that we, thanks to the grace of God, have seen the light. All of us were – as in the words of the hymn of *Amazing Grace* – once blind, but now we see.

But this scripture is really challenging, isn't it, because it calls us to be joyful, prayerful and thankful in *all* circumstances! Most of us have been through trials, big and small, and have scars from the journey. It may really feel that it's beyond our capacity as a human being to be glad, joyful or thankful at all. Right now it might be downright impossible and the right and only thing to do is to cry out in our pain "Lord, where are you?" or "Father God, Why?" Do you know what? If that's how you feel right now, go ahead. It's okay! You see, we are called first and foremost to be honest before our God.

Even with that said, this scripture is also a very practical one and it is helpful whatever circumstance we happen to be in. We are encouraged to "hold onto the good." That good is faith in Jesus Christ. You see, at the end of the day it isn't about you or me at all, it's about Him. This word tells us that "The One who calls you is faithful and He will do it" (v 24). I don't have to muster up thanks and joy, and neither do you. We can get it from Him. His light shines even on the most dismal of days, even in the most dire of circumstances. He is faithful and always will be. He did not desert us on 9/11 or when the December 26 tsunami hit, though it surely felt like it.

And that, I believe, was the secret of Lucia's success. She did die for her faith, but God lived up to His name: Emmanuel, God with us. His light shone not only for her but in her. By all accounts she was burnt alive, so her death was not quick or painless, but she died carrying the unshakable belief that Jesus was "the **light** of the **world**." And she knew, without a shadow of doubt, that whoever followed Him would not walk in darkness, but would have the **light** of life. (paraphrased from John 8:12)

In our church a December or two ago at a family workshop, we turned off all the lights. Even though it was only 3:00 or 4:00 in the afternoon and our church building is in the city, it was pretty gloomy. There was almost no light. Then we lit one large candle. As each of the children came forward to light a candle from the main one, the light in the room grew brighter and brighter. It was a very practical reminder that the spirit of Christ that lives in each of us, shines even on the darkest of days, and when we come together it shines even more brightly. We may not be called to die for our faith like Lucia was, but we are called to "Live as children of light and find out what pleases the Lord" (Ephesians 5:8, 10). Part of what pleases the Lord is not living in isolation, but in community. A community that is not only with Him, but with each other, because there we can be a support and a light even in the darkest of circumstances.

Lord, show us what pleases You. Help us to see the world in which we live though Your eyes. Help us not be so caught up in the busyness of this time of year, but this year, this Christmas time, let us be a ray of light to those whom we come in contact with. Amen.

Lorna

December 14

And Mary said, 'My soul magnifies the Lord, and my spirit rejoices in God my Savior, for he has looked with favor on the lowliness of his servant. Surely, from now on all generations will call me blessed.'

Luke 1:46-48 (NRSV)

A couple in a tiny, darkened room - he is pacing. She is sitting in a thin gown. This moment has been twenty weeks in the making.

Twenty weeks and seven years.

This is their first.

She lies back— the big screen on her right, the table underneath, her husband at her feet...he is fidgeting. She cranes to see the screen but the angle is too great. "Lie back," she is told as an instrument is swept across her.

Excited silence fills the room.

The technician sweeps and then taps on the keyboard; sweeps and then taps, sweeps and taps. She lies there wondering, "Boy or girl... boy or girl?"

The sweeping and the tapping continue.

Slowly she realizes it has gone on for too long. The technician's face is too stiff. Dread creeps into the room. The excitement that once was is now scattered like leaves blown by the harsh, cruel wind of reality.

He no longer paces, but stares.

A doctor comes and fills the tiny room. He too stares at the screen, taps the buttons, and sweeps back and forth, back and forth. Without breathing she puts a voice to her fears. The answer is cold and final.

    No heartbeat.
        No movement.
            No life.

It is called the valley. Although the familiar Psalm reminds us that the Lord is our shepherd through the valley...it is still the valley. It is often dark, often cold, often lonely...and the light–no matter how much we believe in that light–is very hard to see.

We can only assume that Mary had been in the valley.

Poor.
    Unwed.
        Pregnant.

She meets with Elizabeth and Mary's psalm becomes a proclamation of God's eternal goodness. It speaks of what God has done for her. It speaks of what God will do for others.

Those who are poor and powerless.
    Those who are lonely and cold.
        Those who are broken.

Mary proclaims what God will do for those in the valley.

For the Mighty One has done great things for me, and holy is his name. His mercy is for those who fear him from generation to generation. He has shown strength with his arm; he has scattered the proud in the thoughts of their hearts. He has brought down the powerful from their thrones, and lifted up the lowly; he has filled the hungry with good things, and sent the rich away empty (49-53).

We will not always celebrate God's victory in this earthly realm. Eternal joy is the promise. Earthly standards can only truly be set on their head in the heavenly kingdom.

Mary gives us a glimpse at this heavenly kingdom. Those in the valley can follow her voice up toward the heavens and be confident in what God will do.

He has helped his servant Israel, in remembrance of his mercy, according to the promise he made to our ancestors, to Abraham and to his descendants forever (54-55).

A couple in a tiny, darkened room - he is pacing. She is sitting in a thin gown. This moment has been twenty weeks in the making.

Twenty weeks, eight years and one heartbreak.

This is their second.

She lies back— the big screen on her right, the table underneath, her husband at her feet...He is staring at the blank screen, waiting for it to come to life. She cranes to see the screen but the angle is too great. "Lie back," she is told as the instrument is swept across her.

The technician sweeps and then taps on the keyboard; sweeps and then taps some more. She lies there hoping, "Please, please, please…" The sweeping and the tapping continue. Has it gone on for too long? The monitor is turned her way…

>Strong heartbeat.
>>Feel the movement.
>>>The gift of life.

Most gracious Lord, Father and Mother of us all, keep us mindful of your presence both in the depths and in the heights. Open our ears and our hearts to Mary's song; a reminder that this time of year is in preparation and anticipation of the joy that is to be found in your eternal kingdom. May the blessings from you keep us in joy and move us towards deeds of justice and lives of peace. In Your Son's most precious name, Amen.

Will Smama

December 15

There was a man sent from God, whose name was John. He came as a witness to testify to the light, so that all might believe through him. He himself was not the light, but he came to testify to the light.

This is the testimony given by John when the Jews sent priests and Levites from Jerusalem to ask him, 'Who are you?' He confessed and did not deny it, but confessed, 'I am not the Messiah.' And they asked him, 'What then? Are you Elijah?' He said, 'I am not.' 'Are you the prophet?' He answered, 'No.' Then they said to him, 'Who are you? Let us have an answer for those who sent us. What do you say about yourself?' He said, 'I am the voice of one crying out in the wilderness, "Make straight the way of the Lord,"' as the prophet Isaiah said. Now they had been sent from the Pharisees. They asked him, 'Why then are you baptizing if you are neither the Messiah, nor Elijah, nor the prophet?' John answered them, 'I baptize with water. Among you stands one whom you do not know, the one who is coming after me; I am not worthy to untie the thong of his sandal.' This took place in Bethany across the Jordan where John was baptizing.

John 1:6-8, 19-28 (NRSV)

John was sent by God. But still the priests and Levites asked him who he was. They didn't want to know his name or where he grew up. They wanted to know why *he* could preach to *them*. They wanted his credentials. They wanted to know what authority he had. First, they want to know if he is the Messiah – and wouldn't that be a great thing to take back to Jerusalem! They could let everyone know that the Messiah was here and now. But no... John isn't the Messiah. Next best thing: Elijah. Can't you just see it: they really want to have something good, something really news-worthy to take home with them.

But John isn't Elijah either. But maybe he is the prophet. That would still be a pretty good tale. So they put the question to him, and this time the answer is a simple 'no.' I think that John was pretty tired of the questions by that point. Every time they ask whether he is this person or that, his answers get shorter and shorter still. He's probably annoyed with all the pestering, and frustrated that the message is lost because of their obsession with who he is. But then they ask him an open-ended question, and John can tell them who he is.

But they're not done questioning John yet. The Pharisees sent them, we know now. John isn't playing by the rules they've laid out. They want every thing to be exactly correct and in order. They've got to have the details right: Why does John baptize if he doesn't have the right authority, if he isn't the Messiah, Elijah, or the prophet? Their focus on the details of authority and qualifications has drowned out the message that John brings from God. The story recounted here is about authority, and it is replayed in our own lives in much the same way.

We are a credentialed society: we have degrees, certifications, recognitions, honors, and expertise all marked by visible symbols. We have culturally conditioned ways of signaling what our qualifications are and understanding the symbols used by others. This can be good in many ways: I'll admit that I like knowing my doctor is qualified to treat me, that teachers have credentials, and that the policeman knows how to fire his weapon safely. These are all good things. This passage speaks to the risk of letting our concern for qualifications rule our lives.

We want our clergy to have credentials, too. We want to be sure that we're listening to the right person, the one with authority and wisdom. We want assurances. God, however, so often speaks through the least likely, the least qualified, and the least respected. Even though we limit what we're willing to hear, God doesn't limit what is said. God doesn't let qualifications get in the way of His message. When we're consumed by discerning who has authority from who doesn't, we're risking losing out on the message God has for us and the people God sends into our lives.

At the same time, we have to remember not to limit what God does with *us*. How many times I've said to God, "You can't possibly have it right. There's no way *I* can do this.. I don't know how, I don't know anything about it. There are so many people who would be wonderful at this, and you're asking me?? What on *earth* are you thinking?!?" In those moments, God is calling me to remember John in the wilderness. He is calling me to remember that all I need to do His work is the faith to try. He is reminding me that even when I falter, He is with me. When we as a community falter, He is with us always. God calls us to imagine what we can do, to imagine what we can't possibly do, and to trust that He qualifies the called, that He will grace our lives and work with what we need to answer our calling, if we just have enough faith to step out into the unknown and frightening.

John didn't have the qualifications that the priests and Levites were looking for: he wasn't the Messiah, Elijah, or the prophet. But he spoke about the light, the Word who was with God, as God had called him to do. This passage asks us to listen to the voice of God, who calls us every day to newness of life and to His work in the world. By remembering the example of John, who baptized in the desert wilderness, we can better discern God working through others and through us.

Loving God, we are so focused on the minute, the details, and the trivial that we have lost sight of your work in the world and in our lives. Help us to listen for your call, open our eyes to your presence in the most unlikely of people and places, and guide our discernment of your will for us. Remind us of your grace in our successes and our failures as we seek to fulfill our callings to the best of our ability, through Jesus Christ, our Lord, Amen.

Jennifer

December 16

For the grace of God has appeared, bringing salvation to all, training us to renounce impiety and worldly passions, and in the present age to live lives that are self-controlled, upright, and godly, while we wait for the blessed hope and the manifestation of the glory of our great God and Savior, Jesus Christ. He it is who gave himself for us that he might redeem us from all iniquity and purify for himself a people of his own who are zealous for good deeds.
Titus 2:11-14 (NRSV)

As a Benedictine sister, I am immediately struck by how much this passage from Titus parallels the teachings laid out for us in the Rule of Benedict[5], as both texts reflect our lives in the immediate face of the grace of God appearing in the tangible stories of the nativity. But what a closer look at these readings can help us do is to see this training as a life-long lesson and not as a one-day workshop. After all, when the angel said, "For unto you a child is born," he didn't just mean that one day. If we can recognize that God is constantly gifting us with the grace of his son, then perhaps one day we will be able to find ourselves, as Benedict puts it, "running on the path of God's commandments, our hearts overflowing with the inexpressible delight of love."[6] Then we too may want nothing more than a gift that we can immediately give to another, finding in ourselves the simple joy and compassion of a child.

Several years ago, when my oldest nephew was maybe 5 or 6, my brother and I asked him what he got for Christmas. When he mentioned "baby blocks," we grinned at one another and went to find my sister to ask if Santa got "confused" while labeling gifts. Turns out, though, that the only mistake made was by my brother and me,

---

[5] All references to the Rule are taken from Timothy Fry's translation as published by The Liturgical Press in 1982.
[6] Rule of Benedict Prologue, verse 49.

when we passed an automatic judgment on the situation. Apparently, when my sister asked him what he wanted, my nephew began describing some Lion King game. As my sister began to recognize it, she pointed out that he already *had* that game. "But then I can give it to someone else who *doesn't* have it." When she finally was able to get a Christmas list out of him, it had only three items on it: a stuffed tiger, a (different) Lion King game, and something he could give to his 6-month-old baby sister. Out of the mouths of babes...

We often speak of "the innocence of a child." We use that phrase, referring to the purity of children before they become corrupted by "the world." There is, in fact, a story of the little girl alone with her baby brother, asking him to remind her about God, because she's beginning to forget. That's the problem. As we move more and more into the world, we lose sight of God, of the big picture, of what really matters. Christmas, despite the commercialism, has the power to take us out of the world. We get caught up in the spirit of the season, joyously awaiting the arrival of that special day when, if nothing else, we can relive our youth vicariously through our children. While it is, in reality, a time of stress and "stuff"–even in the midst of that there is grace. It's a season of giving, whether to you best friend from college or the Salvation Army bucket. There's an electricity in the air, a time of holiday greetings to strangers on the street that you'd otherwise ignore. Christmas caroling. Secret Santas. Baking cookies. Being of good cheer. All the things that cause visions of sugarplums to dance in our heads, and make the Grinch's small heart grow three sizes this day.

Christmas is a time of transformation, where even the most mean and crass individuals can't help but be touched at least a *tiny* bit. Look at all the stories— Scrooge, the Grinch, *It's a Wonderful Life*— heck, even *The Best Christmas Pageant Ever*. It's a season of conversion. But, unlike Lent, the conversion of Christmas is not "intentional." We don't set out at the beginning of Advent and make active resolutions to become a new creation; it's not something we work at. The conversion of Christmas is subtle, insinuating itself ever-so-slyly such that we don't even notice it's happening. We merely get caught up in the moment. The joy of the anticipation is so great, it would take an active effort *not* to feel a little more charitable, a little more friendly, a little more "other"-focused. It's amazing to see the impact that one guy in a red suit can have on people, religious or not.

But the big day comes and the big day goes, and with it goes everything else. It's the night before Christmas and all through the house, not a creature is stirring, not even a mouse. But the day after Christmas, it's off to the mall, to use up our gift cards and trade in our haul. Why is that? How can something that seems so genuine and sincere one day prove to be nothing but a fleeting memory the next? We go through this every year–why doesn't it stick?

Obviously, the transient nature of holiday cheer is not merely a modern phenomenon. Fifteen hundred years ago, Saint Benedict wrote "a little rule for beginners,"[7] in which he sought to "establish a school for the Lord's service."[8] The Benedictine way of life is built on the idea of daily conversion; one of the three vows professed by a Benedictine is "fidelity to the monastic way of life." But, to borrow from an old ad campaign ... it's not just for monks anymore. The very moderate, very reasonable understanding of human nature displayed in the Rule of Benedict has led to a mass influx of books with such subjects as "The Rule of Benedict for Parents" or "Benedict in Business." We need daily conversion because we (and Benedict includes himself in this) are "slothful, unobservant, and negligent."[9] But if we stay in the struggle and persevere–"Always we begin again" –*that's* what's important.

Our need for daily transformation, and our inability to do it for ourselves, shows up constantly throughout Benedict's Rule. "What is not possible to us by nature, let us ask the Lord to supply by the help of his grace."[10] No, it's not easy. Yeah, we are going to goof up. But we need to keep at it. Ongoing conversion. Our world today doesn't like ideas like that. We think it's a one-time shot–we do it, good, we're done. But it doesn't work like that. We fall down, we get up. We fall again, get back up, only to fall once more. To the world, that seems absurd and pointless. But, as Benedict says: "Your way of acting should be different from the world's way; the love of Christ must come before all else."[11] He speaks of a workshop, humility, "The Tools For Good Works."[12] There is the good zeal, "which separates from evil and leads to God and everlasting life [wherein] no one is to

---

[7] RB 73:8
[8] RB Prol:45
[9] RB 73:7
[10] RB Prol:41
[11] RB 4:20-21
[12] The title of Chapter 4 of the Rule.

pursue what he judges better for himself, but instead, what he judges better for someone else."[13] Sounds like the giving of Christmas to me. At least, until you get to the bit about "Let them prefer nothing whatever to Christ."[14] That's where we fall down every Christmas. Is it about Christ, or is it about the holiday? When we celebrate Christmas, are we truly preferring nothing whatever to Christ? If that's the case, then it should stick a whole lot better than it does.

But that's why Benedict calls it a school, a workshop where we toil faithfully at these tasks of humility, kindness, hospitality, good zeal. We're all beginners. We're all learning. It is the grace of God that has brought us here, and the grace of God that will bring us forward.

"Clothed then with faith and the performance of good works, let us set out on this way, with the Gospel for our guide, that we may deserve to see him who has called us to his kingdom."[15]

Loving Creator, help us to understand that we are merely in training, that how we score on one test is far less important than if we are doing our homework every night. Help us find joy in our successes, and get back up and try once more after our failings. Remind us that we are human, and guide us on the path of your commandments. May we carry the spirit of joy, generosity, and good zeal with us as we progress on this journey, and not just until the end of this calendar page. May we grow ever closer to you, and ever more closer to the you that is in each one of us. We ask this through Christ our Redeemer. Amen.

Steph at Narrow at the Outset

---

[13] RB 72:2, 7
[14] RB 72:11
[15] RB Prol:21

December 17

After the king was settled in his palace and the Lord had given him rest from all his enemies around him, he said to Nathan the prophet, 'Here I am, living in a palace of cedar, while the ark of God remains in a tent.' Nathan replied to the king, 'Whatever you have in mind, go ahead and do it, for the Lord is with you.'

That night the word of the Lord came to Nathan, saying:

'Go and tell my servant David, 'This is what the Lord says: Are you the one to build me a house to dwell in? I have not dwelt in a house from the day I brought the Israelites up out of Egypt to this day. I have been moving from place to place with a tent as my own dwelling. Wherever I have moved with all the Israelites, did I ever say to any of their rulers whom I commanded to shepherd my people Israel, 'Why have you not built me a house of cedar?''

"Now then, tell my servant David, 'This is what the Lord Almighty says: I took you from the pasture and from following the flock to be ruler over my people Israel. I have been with you wherever you have gone, and I have cut off all your enemies from before you. Now I will make your name great, like the names of the greatest men of the earth. And I will provide a place for my people Israel and will plant them so that they can have a home of their own and no longer be disturbed. Wicked people will not oppress them anymore, as they did at the beginning and have done ever since the time I appointed leaders over my people Israel. I will also give you rest from all your enemies.

The Lord declares to you that the Lord himself will establish a house for you...Your house and your kingdom will endure forever before me, your throne will be established forever.' "

2 Samuel 7: 1-11, and 16 (NIV):

This promise to David is identified by Walter Brueggemann as "the most crucial theological statement in the Old Testament."[16] Notice that David is not cautioned that this promise depends on his or his descendants' obedience to God. The unconditional promise is a radical departure from the idea that God's blessing on Israel depends on Israel's obedience to His law. God loves David because David has faith in God. In Christian terms, David has been justified by faith.

---

[16] *First and Second Samuel*, p.259, **Interpretation Commentary Series**, John Knox Press, 1990.

If God loved David so much, then why didn't he let him build his temple in Jerusalem? Why must that wait on David's son, Solomon?

Up to this time God's presence with the people was symbolized by the Ark of the Covenant, which resided in the Tent of Meeting. The Tent and the Ark were built according to God's instructions as given to Moses by the Hebrews while they were wandering in the desert after leaving Egypt and before entering the Promised Land. Every time the nomads moved to a new camp, the Ark was carried with them by the priests in the way prescribed by the law of Moses, bringing the visible presence of the Lord with them as they traveled. After entering the Promised Land, the Ark still had no permanent home. It was moved around with the people as the conquest of Canaan proceeded. Finally, David brings the Ark from Israel to Jerusalem to unify the country under his rule.

King David's motives for building the temple to house the Ark are decidedly mixed. On the one hand, he sincerely wants to honor God with a building intended to glorify Him. On the other hand, building a temple in Jerusalem to house the Ark bolsters his authority by making the presence of God a permanent fixture in the king's capitol city. Therefore, God decrees that Solomon will build the temple, but that King David's house and kingdom will "endure forever before me." King David cannot build the temple and glorify himself. Solomon will build the temple so that God will be glorified and his purpose fulfilled.

God's promise to King David survived the destruction of the temple built and the disappearance of the Ark of the Covenant a couple of centuries later. The Hebrews returned to Jerusalem after 70 years in Babylon, rebuilt the temple and reclaimed their covenant with God. King David's descendants were no longer a royal house as foreign kingdoms ruled Israel. But his house continued to endure in the sight of the Lord until the greatest Son of David, Jesus Christ, the Messiah, was born.

In Jesus, the word of God, contained in the Old Testament, became flesh and lived with us. Jesus embodies God's unconditional love, the same love that God expressed in his promise to King David. That love is not dependent on our good works, our exact observance of God's law, or our perfect faith because Jesus' sacrifice on the cross atoned for our sins. We are now saved by the grace of God in Jesus Christ and look forward to his coming.

Dear Lord, we look for your presence in church buildings and services and forget to look for you at home, in school, at work, at play and in our daily lives. We forget that you are not confined to one place, but that you are with us everywhere. Thank you for your promise to David that his house would endure in your sight. Thank you for your promise to us through the grace of our Lord, Jesus Christ, so we, too, may endure in your sight. Be with us as we anticipate the coming of the Son of David during this Advent season. Amen.

Quotidian Grace

December 18

When Elizabeth heard Mary's greeting, the child leaped in her womb. And Elizabeth was filled with the Holy Spirit and exclaimed with a loud cry, 'Blessed are you among women, and blessed is the fruit of your womb...'

Luke 1:41-42 (NRSV)

Several Advent seasons ago, I was undeniably, unambiguously pregnant. Since I was not yet a pastor, I was able to spend that season anonymously, in the candlelit pew, pondering the incredible journey Mary made to Bethlehem—her ankles swelling and back throbbing—and pondering, of course, the incredible journey laid out before me as well.

I wish that I had a dollar for every time people would say to me, "Your whole life is about to change," a twinkle in their sleep-deprived eye. It's such a silly thing to say, really—what is one supposed to do with that information? Get ready for it? How is that even possible? Nonetheless, I came to realize that I needed to find a way to navigate this transition. But how?

I wonder whether Mary was looking for a way through the transition. After the angel departed, his words still ringing in the air, did Mary decide it was time to take action too?

Because really, what is "Nothing will be impossible with God," but a more theological way of saying, "Your whole life is about to change"?

What is, "The Holy Spirit will come upon you," but an obliteration of any notion of control?

Many sermons have been preached and ink spilled over whether Mary had a choice to let her whole life change, or not. Those questions don't interest me right now. What interests me is that, after the deed is done, after the angel lays out the whole life-changing agenda, after Mary says, "Here I am, the slave of the Lord," she flees the scene.

Of course, she's not running away. She's running *toward*. Mary sets out "with haste" for Elizabeth's house. Once she arrives, the words of greeting are barely out of her mouth before Elizabeth is shouting with utter delight, saying,

> Blessed are you among women!
> Blessed is the child that you carry.
> Blessed are you, who *believed*.

In these words of blessing, Elizabeth testifies that yes, Mary's "whole life is about to change," but
> what does not change,
>> what cannot change,
>>> what will not change,

is God's goodness and mercy.

God's steadfast love endures forever, which is to say, it endures any circumstance of life that might befall us. Certainly Mary, as she prepared to become a wife and a mother simultaneously, needed that blessing.

And certainly I, too, needed to hear the good news that lasts. Everything changes, but our loving God does not. And so, like Mary, I ran.

I ran to the company of others who could help me make sense of this change, who could affirm the goodness of God. Those others were trusted women who gave me a tremendous gift—a gift called a Blessingway.

A Blessingway is believed to be rooted in the Navajo tradition. My Blessingway consisted of fifteen women who gathered for the sole purpose of marking this transition in my life. They shared stories, offered experiences, dispensed wisdom, and gave me words of blessing for the journey into motherhood.

First, the group wrote an impromptu song for me—a lullaby about the peace and comfort of God.

They each brought a word that represented a gift they wished to share with me—words like simplicity, grace, humor and unconditional love.

They laid hands on me and prayed for a healthy birth. And they accepted candles from me and agreed to light them when I went into labor, as a way of holding me in prayer.

I will never forget the gift of that time. As I sat in that place, soaking up the blessing (because what else can one do but simply receive it?), I knew that the significance of their blessing would only deepen over time. Years later, I still sing the song of peace to my daughter. I read my friends' words of encouragement when I'm feeling off balance and uncertain. Mostly I remember the warmth of sitting among them. The blessing continues.

I can't help but see threads of the Blessingway in the encounter between Mary and Elizabeth. Here are two women, each on the verge of cataclysmic change, reaching out to one another and finding refuge and strength—Elizabeth, graced by the presence of Mary; and Mary, lifted up in the blessing that bubbles forth from Elizabeth, and moved to sing her own song of faith and joy. And I feel certain that, over the course of Mary's life, those words of blessing brought her comfort. In moments of exhaustion and exasperation (surely she had them), in times of confusion, and perhaps even in that moment of unspeakable grief which is the stuff of nightmares for any parent—that blessing was an anchor. It was a place of orientation: No matter what happened, she was God's own.

But if I may be so bold, I believe that Elizabeth's blessing was more than a word of comfort. I think Elizabeth's blessing *called Mary into being* as a mother. After all, Elizabeth's words were a gift of the Holy Spirit, the same Spirit who empowered Mary to conceive and carry this child in the first place! We dare not try to separate these two events; they are both actions of the Spirit and, I believe, inextricably linked to one another.

> The words we share with one another matter.
> The blessings we offer to one another matter.
> How can we believe otherwise and still worship a God
> who *spoke* the world into being?

As I left my Blessingway that night so long ago, I knew deeply that I was ready. Not in the sense of being prepared. Not in the sense of knowing what to expect. No, through their blessings my friends *called me into being* as a mother. Their blessings made it so! I cannot explain it. I simply know it. I *became* a mother even as I was still *becoming* a mother.

And that is the power of the blessing. I cannot separate the naming of the experience from the experience itself—not for me, and not for Mary. Elizabeth saw Mary for who she already was and yet still was growing to be. My friends celebrated my journey even as they cheered my arrival.

And it is there, somewhere between being and becoming, somewhere amidst change and transition and Advent expectancy, that the blessing lies. It is a gift of the Spirit, and it waits for us— to find it, to name it for one another, and to allow it to change us.

Spirit of the living God, who spoke the world into being and called it good—give me ears to hear the quiet, life-giving blessings of this season, and the words to share words of blessing with others. Amen.

reverendmother

December 19

In the sixth month of Elizabeth's pregnancy, God sent the angel Gabriel to Nazareth, a town in Galilee, to a virgin pledged to be married to a man named Joseph, a descendant of David. The virgin's name was Mary. The angel went to her and said, 'Greetings, you who are highly favored! The Lord is with you.'"

Luke 1: 26 – 28 (TNIV)

Fra Angelico created this image in the 15th century.[17] We were introduced on my 18th birthday at a museum in Cortona, Italy, but our relationship didn't end there- it was just beginning. My art teacher (a.k.a. the-coolest-chaperone-ever) bought me a copy to bring home. This was before college. Long before seminary. Eons before marriage and motherhood would seat themselves on my front porch and ask to be invited in. This picture has traveled with me through it all.

So much has changed, but this has not: what I loved about this painting then is what I still love about it, the way that the words of the angel take on a life of their own. They are SO real. SO important. SO Divine. They cannot help but become visual and golden as they leap off of the angel's tongue.

Every time I look at them I am like my daughter the first time she saw the acolyte light the candle to signal the start of worship- mouth open, giddy with excitement, sure that something amazing is about to happen.

And it is. Of course the words of Gabriel are golden! What else could they be? They are carrying a message from God.

---

[17] Fra Angelico, Annunciation. 1433-34. Tempera on wood, 150 x 180 cm. Museo Diocesano, Cortona

Ironically, my favorite poem about the Annunciation is exactly the opposite. It isn't lofty or golden at all, but noticeably down to earth as it describes what Gabriel might have felt as he prepared to propose God's plan to Mary.

> "She is sitting near the window, doing nothing, unaware of his presence. How beautiful she is. He gazes at her as a man might gaze at his beloved wife sleeping beside him....Ah: wasn't there something he was supposed to say?...Yes, yes, he will remember the message, in a little while."[18]

Maybe this is why I love Advent so much, maybe even more than Christmas. The Lofty and the Ordinary aren't married yet, but they've started dating. And it's that sweet part of a relationship where everything seems just perfect. Angel and mortal. Minister and brewer. AIDS orphan and billionaire. The two ends of the spectrum not only meet, they find out that they genuinely care about and need each other.

Here's what we know. As long as it's God's plan, Mary is in. Joseph decides (after another angelic intervention) to stick with Mary. Herod isn't slaughtering. Temple watchers aren't gossiping. Mary probably can't even imagine that one day this son that she took such a risk to welcome would say that she was not his mother.

I wonder if, in later years, they looked back with regret? Wondered if they should have pushed a little more to find out what it means, precisely, to be favored by God?

But those are not the questions for now. For now we just need to savor this moment. This moment when God made a request and a Child of God said yes. This moment when words became both golden and visible and filled the imaginations and hopes of all people who were tired of tears.

I believe that the Words of God still become golden and visible. Do we see them?

I know we still need them. Need the words of God to be not just words on a page but alive, pregnant, with possibility.

---

[18] *The Gospels In Our Image: An Anthology of Twentieth-Century Poetry Based on Biblical Texts.* David Curzon, Editor. Harcourt & Brace, 1995.

We need them and God is inviting us to speak them. Words of caring. Hope. Compassion. Truth spoken with love. There's food enough for all!

We are all being called to speak these things in the most traditional way possible-with our lives.

One Who Spoke, One Who Is Speaking, We pray for listening. Lives vulnerable to your grace. We are thank-full for the ways in which your words weave a tapestry of hope and possibility, promise and forgiveness. We are thank-full for your favor, calling us to be servants. Help us to abandon the blinders that keep us from seeing your words alive in the world. We're looking for courage enough to share them. Amen.

apstraight

December 20

Then Jesus cried out, "When a man believes in me, he does not believe in me only, but in the one who sent me. When he looks at me, he sees the one who sent me. I have come into the world as a light, so that no one who believes in me should stay in darkness."

John 12: 44-46 (NIV)

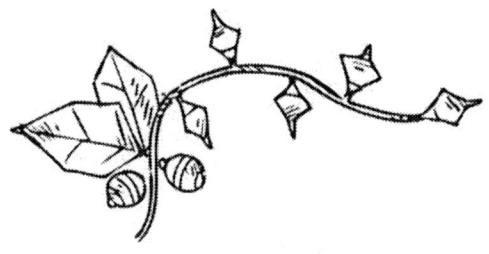

When most of us think about the Christmas season we conjure up warm, fuzzy memories from Christmases past. We smile as we wrap our presents, knowing they will bring joy to our loved ones. We tell stories and drink hot cocoa, sharing with the little ones our knowledge of how Santa gets to all the houses in one night or how he fits that big fat belly down that skinny little fireplace. We mail out our holiday cards to both friends and family, some of whom we realize we haven't connected with in quite some time. We bake cookies and candy and make our seasonal promise to ourselves that we'll go back around to dieting when the pumpkin pie is gone. We put up the Christmas tree and then stand back to marvel that each year it seems to be more beautiful than the last. We reminisce about the history of our families as we carefully extract all the special heirloom ornaments that we've collected throughout the years, recalling the special memories that seem to be float out from our minds as we carefully hang each one upon the tree.

I always remember the set of bubble lights that used to be on my grandparents' tree each year. They were shaped like an old-fashioned candlestick, with a half-rounded base at the bottom and a little glass globe that looked like a small thermometer on the top. Inside each one was a different colored liquid that, as the electricity began heating up the strand of lights, would cause the lights to begin to bubble and I, a child not yet in her double-digit years, always thought it looked like... *magic.*

The year I turned twenty-one, we lost my grandmother to cancer and from that point on, my grandfather stopped putting up a Christmas tree. He said it was "a lot of trouble to go to for such a short amount of time." I think it was more that he couldn't stand to take those lights out of their box each year, knowing Grandma wouldn't be there to see our faces as the tree would begin to dance with its colored lights and bubbles. One year he told me we should take them home with us for our tree; he needn't be bothered with such things anymore, especially now that he was moving to a smaller house.

I remember fearing that my Grandfather's world would soon grow dark without the glow of that old strand of bubble lights.

But, we did as he wished and we put those lights on our family tree for the next several years. However, we noticed with each passing Christmas, they became more and more worn, and one by one the bulbs began to break or the liquid would leak out. Eventually, there was no good reason to even take the strand out of the box again. Now all that was left was just the childhood memory of those wonderful, bubbling, magical lights.

A few years later, my Grandfather started to join us at my house each Christmas, along with the rest of my family who would migrate back to our family home like a gaggle of Canadian Geese. He continued to do so right up until his very last Christmas in 1998. Out of my four grandparents, he was the last one I would have to say goodbye to, and he was by far the toughest one for me to finally release.

He was the sweetest old man, never without a Brach's candy in his pocket and a tickle or two tucked up his sleeve. He would have my mother dress us all up when we were little so he could parade us around the Courthouse (where he worked as County Clerk) to show everyone his beautiful, well-mannered grandchildren. He took us fishing at the lake and even taught us how to drive a ball on the greens at his ritzy country club. He'd make us home-churned vanilla ice cream in the summer and then top it off with fresh red raspberries that he'd plucked right off his own bushes. He'd spend hours passing the time showing us his coin collection complete with real gold certificates and his favorite inkwells that he collected in homage to his past. In the evenings, he'd smoke a cigar from a big white box that smelled like someone had caught a cherry tree on fire. I loved that smell and would sit below his feet watching the smoke rings float up to the ceiling.

I was overwhelmed with sadness the day we buried him, and a part of me felt like some of my "light" went out that day as well.

Then, last year, I went through a medical crisis that precipitated one of the worst bouts of depression I have ever known.

For six months I was literally in a fight for my life, day in and day out. At the end of it all, when I knew I couldn't take another day of living the empty life I had built for myself, I finally broke down and begged God to come and save me from myself. He graciously did just that. Just because I asked, he came down and pulled me back to safety and the following morning I *knew* something life altering had happened to me the night before. After weeks of lying around in mental darkness, afraid to face not only myself but the mess I had made of my life, I now suddenly seemed to be on fire with the light of Jesus Christ. I had become that strand of Christmas lights from years and years ago… bubbling with the secrets that I now held inside me and knowing that my life was truly…*magic*.

Dear Heavenly Father, we ask that as we go throughout this holiday season, you remind us all to stop and reflect on where we would be had Your Son never come to earth to light up our world with his presence. Where there are those whose lives seem dark and who feel "burned out," we ask that you shine your grace down upon their lives. And, Father, for those of us whose lives are more than we had ever hoped they could be, we pray that you will use us at Your will to spread our light to those who cannot see. In Jesus' name I pray. Amen.

HeyJules

December 21

For I am persuaded, that neither death, nor life, nor angels, nor principalities, nor powers, nor things present, nor things to come, Nor height, nor depth, nor any other creature, shall be able to separate us from the love of God, which is in Christ Jesus our Lord.
Romans 8:38-39 (KJV)

Last year, a week before Christmas or so, my children and I were out and about looking at the bright lights and decorations and Christmas shopping. I had begun to think about the images of Christmas. I thought about and still think about the public, common images and icons of Christmas—the mall, presents, lights, Santa, silver bells and good smells. And there are expectations about what one should do at Christmas—we are supposed to be wrapping presents, decorating cookies, sitting by a roaring fire roasting chestnuts and marshmallows, singing carols and sharing a cup of cheer. And yet…

Tonight is the longest night of the year. The sun has been slipping further and further south every day for weeks until we dwell in darkness 15 and 16 hours a day. The trees have lost all their leaves and their limbs sketch a black trace work against a grey and darkening sky. There is a dank coldness to the air—the wind blows and chills us to the bone. The world is grey and dark and foreboding. Yet we hear from our car radios that this is the "Hap, happiest time of the year"—the most wonderful season of all. There is glitter and tinsel and bright lights strung about, in seeming defiance of the gloom of the world.

And the truth is, the world is a dark and foreboding place for many of us. For months the color has been leaking out of our world, the green of summer is gone, the colors of the autumn leaves have blown away, and the world is grey and black. Our days are shorter, our nights are longer, the air is colder and the skies are cloudier. And we start thinking, "Another new year is almost here—did I do all I needed to do? Did I do all I wanted to do? What have I done with my life? Has it been worth it? I listen and I hear singing—Joy to the World—are we all full of Joy? Where is the Joy?"

There is no Joy for the man who has lost his wife of 50 years this last summer. There is no Joy for the single mother who was downsized again and cannot feed her children. There is no Joy when there is a new empty chair at the dinner table. There is no Joy when you don't even know how you are paying for the rent and utilities, much less presents for the kids. There is no Joy when your husband packs up and says that he is leaving. There is no Joy for the woman who is dying of cancer, for the man with no family. There is no Joy when your son calls and says that he is under fire every night in Iraq. There is no Joy for those who have lost livelihood and family and home to a thundering storm. There is no Joy when your city lays under 20 feet of toxic water. There is no Joy. Not for everyone.

At the beginning of every Sunday in our church, we sing "O come, O come, Emmanuel, And ransom captive Israel, That mourns in lonely exile here, Until the Son of God appear." And we mourn. And we sit in our loneliness. And we pray "O come, Thou Day-spring, come and cheer, Our spirits by Thine advent here; Disperse the gloomy clouds of night, And death's dark shadows put to flight." So often we sit in our private darkness and we pretend. We put on the happy face for our kids, for our parents, our friends, because we don't want to spoil Christmas. We go around hiding our pain, sometimes even from ourselves. Yet we mourn. Advent is a dark time of year. Yet true darkness is more than the absence of light; true darkness is being alone and suffering. Being alone and in pain is the real darkness. Darkness exists and thrives when you can't really talk about your pain and share it with others.

Yet, wasn't if dark that first Christmas? The story is not a bright and happy one. It's a story of a teenager's unexpected pregnancy, an upset and angry man who is not the father of the child. It's a story of an oppressive government who is forcing taxation on a poor and subdued society. It's a story of overcrowding – of a birth in an animal stall. It's a story of parents too poor to afford the usual sacrifice at Temple. It's a story of a family forced to flee to Egypt because of a deranged ruler. It's a story of a baby born to die.

And yet all things do work together for good.[19] It's also a story of a generous man who marries a young girl carrying a baby not his.

---

[19] Romans 8:28

Of unexpected generosity by three men who could be kings. Of a child who grew up favored God. Of a generous God who provides for his people. Of a God working through events most would call overwhelming. God brought light into the world on the world's darkest night. And that light shines still among us. As we sit in our own darkness we can remember this and begin to hope that God will take these strands of light and darkness, of suffering and of joy and interweave them together to make a tapestry out of our lives–and one of beauty in spite of the pain.

After tonight, the days will begin to become longer and the nights shorter. The light will begin to grow and the darkness will diminish. With the birth of the Christ child, light comes back into our world and this light is a beacon of hope for us. We find that light to be a lamp unto our feet and a light unto our path. God is with us— Emmanuel. He shall be called Wonderful, Counselor, Prince of Peace. Jesus knows this darkness. He was "despised and rejected of men; a man of sorrows, and acquainted with grief."[20] He knows our pain. One great theologian reminds us that we cannot come to the manger without acknowledging that it lies in the shadow of the cross. Light came down at Christmas, no more than that–the "Life-Light blazed out of the darkness; the darkness couldn't put it out."[21] Light and Love came down at Christmas–and nothing will be able to separate us from that Love.

Love came down at Christmas,
Love all lovely, love divine;
Love was born at Christmas,
Star and angels gave the sign.

Love shall be our token,
Love shall be yours and love be mine,
Love to God and to all men,
Love for plea and gift and sign.
    — Christina Rossetti

reverend mommy

---

[20] Isaiah 53:3a (KJV)
[21] John 1:5 from *The Message*

December 22

*The people who walked in darkness
have seen a great light;
those who lived in a land of deep darkness—
on them light has shined.
You have multiplied the nation,
you have increased its joy;
they rejoice before you
as with joy at the harvest,
as people exult when dividing plunder.
For the yoke of their burden,
and the bar across their shoulders,
the rod of their oppressor,
you have broken as on the day of Midian.
For all the boots of the tramping warriors
and all the garments rolled in blood
shall be burned as fuel for the fire.
For a child has been born for us,
a son given to us;
authority rests upon his shoulders;
and he is named
Wonderful Counsellor, Mighty God,
Everlasting Father, Prince of Peace.
His authority shall grow continually,
and there shall be endless peace
for the throne of David and his kingdom.
He will establish and uphold it
with justice and with righteousness
from this time onwards and for evermore.
The zeal of the LORD of hosts will do this.*

Isaiah 9:2-7 (NRSV)

A light scandalizes the darkness, and everything is changed. Sorrow is displaced by joy. Despair gives way to hope. Oppression crumbles under the righteous weight of justice. Broken relationships are reconciled, and forgiveness blankets the earth like light blazing from the North Star.

And all because a woman carried an infant for nine months in the holy space of her womb. The ordinary miracle of gestation brings forth a child who is anything but ordinary. The child is an answer to prayer, the fulfillment of a promise—even as he screams with indignation at the trauma of birth. His flesh is spackled with goosebumps. His nose is assailed with the stench of stable animals. His tiny fists grasp the air, searching for the warm walls that protected him since conception. He is bloodied, furious, hungry. He is like every other human child, only he is named Wonderful Counsellor, Mighty God, Everlasting Father, Prince of Peace. He is the light that blazes in the darkness, the infant babe who will grow into a precocious Torah prodigy, and mature into a radical holy man, gifted with the wisdom of God, indeed, gifted with the very Spirit of God. His mother will nurse him, and in turn, he will nurse the whole of Creation with his healing touch.

    This child emerges into a world that is overcast with darkness. It is the midnight of humanity. The sun is elsewhere. The moon is new. The shadows are rendered in such a deep tone of black that sojourners cannot discern the road ahead. Little children marvel that they cannot make out their hands in front of their face. Kings bemoan the danger of darkness, the vulnerability of the night. The wicked revel in nocturnal safety. In the pitch black hours, they can get away with murder. And when a young mother exhausts herself with one final push, a brilliant light saturates the sky with the glory of ten suns, ten thousand lightening bolts, and one hundred thousand candles. Witnesses are blinded by the sight, filled with the warm peace of a new day, delightfully bewildered by the sudden acceleration of joy.

    How is it, then, that this light is so easy to miss? Do I really blink long enough to miss the radiance of this child that is born to us?

    I have spent so many Christmases cowering in the darkness, unable to peel my hands from my face, unwilling to open my eyes to the miracle. I know that the miracle is there to behold. I know that the child is holy. I go to the Christmas Eve service, and I join the circle of worshippers as we sing *Silent Night* by candlelight. But inside I am wincing. I have not prepared for this child. I have not trusted that the light will come out of the darkness. I have joined a great majority in a secular ritual that amounts to running around in the darkness screwing in artificial light bulbs— preparing for the birth of Christ with a credit card and a planner full of parties. It is not so much that I think such festivities are wrong, but I rarely leave room for silence, for anticipation. When the Christmas Eve comes, I realize I haven't lit my Advent candles, haven't kept up with my devotional readings, haven't pondered the very real darkness of a broken world. So I finish wrapping up the last stocking stuffers and resign myself to the silence of sorrow.

But the Lord of Hosts is persistent. One might even echo Isaiah and call our Creator *zealous*. Even if we have ignored the possibility of repentance in years past, we are still invited to fall to our knees before the baby Jesus and weep with joy at his arrival. Even when we have not prepared ourselves for the amazing gift of this child, we are still prodded to receive him. We are still called into a holy embrace with the One called Emmanuel, God-with-us. This holy child, this Prince of Peace, disarms our insistence that we are not worthy to cradle him in our arms and call him Savior.

This Son is truly a gift, and the punch line to God's gift of grace is that we don't have to earn it. The gift is given, freely. The love is poured out. We are disentangled from artificial happiness and guilty despair, and freed to experience the muscular hope of incarnation. Prepared or unprepared, we are equally invited to participate in the midwifery of this great birth.

Wonderful Counsellor, your holy light burns through our fiercest defenses. Open us to the gift of this child, that we might follow him out of the darkness into the Kingdom of God. Amen.

Katherine

December 23

Now to God who is able to strengthen you according to my gospel and the proclamation of Jesus Christ, according to the revelation of the mystery that was kept secret for long ages but is now disclosed, and through the prophetic writings is made known to all the Gentiles, according to the command of the eternal God, to bring about the obedience of faith— to the only wise God, through Jesus Christ, to whom be the glory forever! Amen.

Romans 16:25-27 (NRSV)

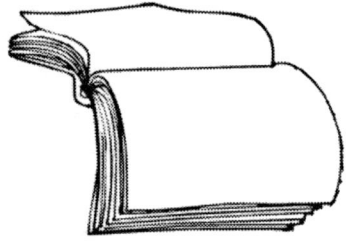

I was once mentor for an intensive group study of Scripture and theology. It seemed as if, at every Friday morning session, as we puzzled over some of the more difficult questions raised by our faith, that more often than not, at the end, we would have to shrug and declare, "it's a mystery!"

How can Jesus be fully human and fully divine? It's a mystery! How could Mary give birth to him even though she was a virgin? It's a mystery! How was Jesus resurrected after three days in the tomb? It's a mystery! Do we in any way earn our salvation or is everything we do completely predestined? It's a mystery!

So, then, according to this ending of Paul's letter to the Romans, we are strengthened by God for obedience in faith—to a mystery.

Well, that's just great. That's really helpful. I've got a last-minute shopping list, huge quantities of ingredients to be assembled into some sort of holiday feast the day after tomorrow, and a Christmas Eve sermon I've been wrestling with all week, and I'm doing all this because of an unanswerable mystery.

My experience is that Christians get ourselves into trouble when we try to answer some of those unanswerable questions. We start drawing those lines between groups of people that at best, harden into denominations, at their worst, have been justification for the slaughter of thousands in wars and persecution. We are all too willing to let our fallible human understanding of the mystery so graciously revealed to us in Jesus Christ define and dictate our relationships with family and friends.

In the tradition of the Episcopal Church, which is my faith home, we recite the Nicene Creed every Sunday. And perhaps, over the years, we've become too accustomed to taking those statements as scientific facts that define whether or not you're a good Christian, as opposed to a body of mysterious ideas that are worth exploring for the rest of your life.

This is so very easy to preach about, so much harder to do. Like many other Episcopalians (and clergywomen), I am a great consumer of mysteries. I wait eagerly for the next Elizabeth George, P.D. James and Tony Hillerman. And then I am totally useless until I get to the conclusion, until the mysteries are revealed, the culprits are found, and the characters and the reader experience justice or closure.

What if we started to understand ourselves as living in the middle of a mystery novel, with the end yet to be revealed? It's all right for us to yearn to get to the ending, to study the clues left for us along the way. We have Scripture and tradition and reason to mine for the revelation that has been disclosed to all of us. But we don't get to rush ahead to the conclusion. Justice and closure are in God's hands; we're characters who get to live in obedience of faith to the best of our abilities, strengthened by the wise God who knows all too well that we humans are not ready yet for the end of the story.

I wonder if living in obedience of faith means seeking out clues to the mystery without making judgments about how it all fits together in the end. I wonder if it means spending some time, in the twelve days of Christmas, which follow on tomorrow's heels, mending relationships that have been broken by our easy willingness to sacrifice love in the name of certainty.

Mary is about to be delivered of the greatest mystery of all. Our job is not to understand it, but to join her in the stable, in the middle of the story, at the invitation of the God who is wise above all our imaginings.

Blessed Trinity, font of all wisdom, we give you praise for all we do not understand. Give us grace to see what you would have us perceive in our time on earth, that we may serve you faithfully, and at the end, join you at the Table prepared for all of us, in the beginning, with your Word. Amen.

Hazelnut Reflections

December 24

In those days a decree went out from Emperor Augustus that all the world should be registered. This was the first registration and was taken while Quirinius was governor of Syria. All went to their own towns to be registered. Joseph also went from the town of Nazareth in Galilee to Judea, to the city of David called Bethlehem, because he was descended from the house and family of David. He went to be registered with Mary, to whom he was engaged and who was expecting a child. While they were there, the time came for her to deliver her child.

Luke 2:1-6 (NRSV)

The players are familiar. We know the shepherds, the wise men, the angels, King Herod, Mary, Joseph, and the baby. When we think of pageants and plays and films and carols we can add a few other characters to the story of Christmas. There must have been an innkeeper to turn Joseph away. There were friendly beasts—that carol is a particular favorite in my family—the faithful shaggy brown donkey, the doves who cooed the baby to sleep, the cow who gave up her manger for his bed. Tonight, as we go to Bethlehem in our hearts, let us take a closer look at those without whom there would be no story. I think their different responses to the events of the first Christmas describe a number of ways we can respond to this Christmas, to have it be as new to us as it was to them and to know ourselves better in the process.

We begin with Mary, young and innocent and supremely faithful to God. She must have been filled with a quiet courage as she traveled the weary road to Bethlehem, to give birth away from home with only a man to help her, rather than the community of women who would ordinarily have surrounded her at a birth. Mary's response to the incarnation, to the coming of God into human form, was receptive and interior. She pondered these things in her heart. To be able to meditate and reflect in this way is a spiritual gift.

Joseph, on the other hand, dealt with the outside world. His faith played out in a more exterior fashion. What needed doing to keep Mary safe? What would her life be like if he **didn't** marry her? Joseph was ready to act and to solve their problems as best he could. He must have been a practical man. Our families and our faith communities need such people. They keep our lights burning and our oil tanks full. They keep our house in order. Theirs is not the most glamorous role, and neither was Joseph's, but they matter very much to the story and to us.

The shepherds remind me of folk who respond from their feelings. The shepherds are impulsive. They hear the message and hurry to see if it is true, and then hurry to share it with others. These people are truly touched by the Good News. They make us want to come to church, to share together and to celebrate. They radiate joy.

Some people are more like the Magi. Faith to them is a matter of study. We need them, too, with their curious minds and questioning, seeking way of approaching a life of faith. They are the students of the word and the interpreters of the symbol. If you imagine yourself to be on a faith journey, you are like one of the Magi.

And of course our cast of characters in Bethlehem tonight includes naysayers as well. When we think of the possible hosts who turned away Mary and Joseph that night, we are in touch with the kind of life that is too busy with worldly things to allow for an awareness of the divine. And King Herod actively seeks to destroy the "king" he fears will dethrone him and his family. We are like him when we hold tightly to old ways out of fear.

We all have the potential for those negative traits, as well as the positive characteristics of reflection, action, emotion, and thought seen in the others in our story of Bethlehem. Each day, not just at Christmas, we choose which of those tendencies will lead us in a life of faith.

If we were in that stable tonight, the animals would surround us. They may teach us to live in the moment, sensing only what is happening right now. And that's the way we want to be on Christmas Eve. We smell the hay. We see the star. We hear the soft sounds of the baby. **We** know that he is the Christ child, God made human being, come to Earth to show us the great love of our Creator for all creation.

O Holy Child of Bethlehem, descend to us we pray. Cast out our sin and enter in, be born in us today. We hear the Christmas Angels the great glad tidings tell. O come to us, abide with us, Our Lord Emmanuel. Amen.

Songbird

December 25

The people who walked in darkness have seen a great light; those who lived in a land of deep darkness— on them light has shined. You have multiplied the nation, you have increased its joy; they rejoice before you as with joy at the harvest, as people exult when dividing plunder. For the yoke of their burden, and the bar across their shoulders, the rod of their oppressor, you have broken as on the day of Midian. For all the boots of the tramping warriors and all the garments rolled in blood shall be burned as fuel for the fire. For a child has been born for us, a son given to us; authority rests upon his shoulders; and he is named Wonderful Counselor, Mighty God, Everlasting Father, Prince of Peace. His authority shall grow continually, and there shall be endless peace for the throne of David and his kingdom. He will establish and uphold it with justice and with righteousness from this time onward and forevermore. The zeal of the LORD of hosts will do this.

Isaiah 9:2-7 (NRSV)

Anyone who has sung Handel's *Messiah* is familiar with this scripture passage, which foretells the coming of the Savior, and His bringing of light to the world. I cannot read it without hearing the music: both the marvelous bass solo "The people that walked in darkness have seen a great light," and the triumphant chorus "For unto us a child is born," with its litany of titles for the Child who comes today.

Handel's music for that bass solo is all ponderous weight in a minor key, while trudging through the desert, feeling lost and forgotten. Then there is a transformation to the major key, and higher range, for the phrase "have seen a great light." The magic of the key shift from minor to major underscores the glory of what we have been given. The major key by itself is no great thing. It's the transition that carries the import of what we are hearing, and what we are living as Christians on this day.

The wonder of the Nativity is embodied and foreshadowed in this text, but to me, an important part of the lesson we learn here is the darkness and its role in making the light so much more glorious.

I think of our beautiful Christmas Eve midnight service, conducted largely by candlelight, a palpable reminder of the power of small light writ large. We sing "Silent Night", knowing that the black sky outside, lit only by stars at this hour, will lead us to a morning of glorious light, and a newborn Savior. I smile, thinking of that service, remembering a Christmas Eve when my preteen son, looking to liven up the evening, started lighting the little pills on his sweater with the candle. Tiny little burst of flame – no more than that, thank goodness – adding to the light in the nave. It was his own childish way of celebrating the light while amusing himself, of course, but a joyful moment nonetheless.

It echoes the Easter vigil service, also conducted in candlelight. The music is not as joyful, because of the memory of the darkness of Good Friday. The need for darkness to precede the light is more obvious at Eastertide. The stark contrast of the sense of despair and loss giving way to triumph and resurrection is clearer, more unambiguous.

And yet, even this Christmas season flickers with dark and light.

The Advent season, when we prepare for Christ's coming, is also the time when the days grow shorter. Darkness dominates, and we long for sunlight. When the sunlight comes, it is thin and cold. We wonder if it will ever be spring, if our bones will ever stop aching, if the trees will ever be anything but gray brown skeletons in the sky.

Without that darkness, without the cold, the glorious light of Jesus' birth would be meaningless.

Many years ago, when my father died, my mother decided that she and I would go somewhere warm for Christmas—Florida, to be exact. It was strange. I was used to the seasons changing, and I was used to hoping for a snow-white Christmas. The day, when it came, seemed oddly disjointed from the Christmas I knew and loved. I needed the cold, the darkness, the waiting and not knowing what was coming and yet knowing what was coming. The harsh sunlight and heat made no sense. Light and warmth were for the day, for the celebration, not for the season. Perhaps it was a failing of mine as a northern girl that I could not appreciate that odd fool's gold of light in the Florida December.

We have expectations of light: when it is appropriate, what it means, where it will shine. We look forward to that thin, struggling sunlight in the early hours of winter mornings—it has been so long since the afternoon before with its easily tiring sun—and the context of that infant morning light helps us appreciate its limited strengths. We appreciate it despite its seeming weakness. It is a portent of the day, a portent of the spring, a portent of brighter times.

Over a decade later, when my first child was due on December 26th, the sense of waiting in a "Cloud of Unknowing" was even more intense. I looked forward to the Christmas celebrations, not knowing if my child would come in the midst of that wonderful celebration, or before, or after. For the record, he was born on January 2nd. I cooked Christmas dinner, and entertained a houseful of relatives, and waited on. But the darkness, the waiting, the wondering were even more real than usual. I was turned inward that week, in communion with my waiting child, with my body as it prepared itself for the labor ahead. The light was yet to come, and it would make no sense without this period of darkness and meditation.

In ancient times, hermits would go live in caves to meditate. Perhaps their choice of caves was for coolness, to get out of the sunlight. I think, though, that their choice might have been for the darkness. Being able to go to a place of quiet and darkness, to commune with God without distraction, must have been a gift of grace in small communities where quiet may have been rare.

They knew that the darkness could teach them to appreciate the light. Waiting could teach them to appreciate the gift. Silence could teach them to appreciate the music.

Thus, I'd suggest on this day of glorious light and music and family, to find a little time to remember and cherish the darkness, for without it, how are we to know and love the light?

In the joyful morning light of new birth, in the delicate candlelight of evening peace and gladness, make me ever mindful, Lord, of this, the greatest of your gifts to us, your incarnate Son. Let me share the joy not only with my family and my friends, but also with the larger community of Your children. Let the peace I feel, the warmth of the light, fill my heart and remind me that You give it to me not to keep, but to share.
Amen.

Rev-to-be-Mibi

December 26

In the beginning was the Word, and the Word was with God, and the Word was God. He was with God in the beginning. Through him all things were made; without him nothing was made that has been made. In him was life, and that life was the light of men. The light shines in the darkness, but the darkness has not understood it. There came a man who was sent from God; his name was John. He came as a witness to testify concerning that light, so that through him all men might believe. He himself was not the light; he came only as a witness to the light. The true light that gives light to every man was coming into the world. He was in the world, and though the world was made through him, the world did not recognize him. He came to that which was his own, but his own did not receive him. Yet to all who received him, to those who believed in his name, he gave the right to become children of God— children born not of natural descent, nor of human decision or a husband's will, but born of God. The Word became flesh and made his dwelling among us. We have seen his glory, the glory of the One and Only, who came from the Father, full of grace and truth.

John 1:1-14 (NIV)

The BBC broadcasts a much loved radio program, Desert Island Discs, which has been running for an incredible 53 years. The format is simple. Each week a celebrity, in the widest definition of the word, is invited to choose the 8 pieces of music, one book (excluding the Bible, Shakespeare and big encyclopedias) which they would wish to have with them in case of shipwreck on a desert island. The "desert island" principle can of course be applied to much else in life, and I suspect that if asked to select one passage of Scripture to last them for a very long time, this amazing prose poem, the Prologue to John's Gospel, would head the list for many people.

Fourteen verses sum up so much, from the cosmic grandeur of creation to the breathtaking immediacy of Christ's birth. Here it is abundantly clear that our God is bent on relationship, on communicating himself with his creation…he is not only a being, but the ***Word***. However, a word (even the Word) can communicate nothing unless there is somebody ready to receive it, to listen or to read…

So for God to be fully Himself, he must be God-in-relationship with Godself—Father, Son and Spirit. God also seeks relationship with us. So there is something close to pathos in our failure to recognize and connect with God:

"*He was in the world, yet the world did not recognize him. He came to that which was his own, but his own did not receive him.*"

It's incredible, isn't it? The One who framed and formed everything, allowing himself to be shut out of his own creation because he wants us to *choose* to know him. He who needs nothing, putting himself in a place where he needs us, *us!*

What kind of God is that?

And, lest the Word be heard once and then forgotten, here He is made real, visible solid flesh.

Incarnate. The Word translates himself into a language we can understand, the language of humanity. The glory of God is too vast for us to comprehend, so He sets it aside, and chooses to limit himself to our scale, so that we might have a chance of recognizing and responding to him. As Irenaeus put it, writing in the first century of the Church, "He became what we are, to make us what he is."

What's more, John's prologue does not just look back to the dawn of time, nor confine us to the historic realities of first century Palestine. It sweeps through the centuries, reminding us that in every place, every time, "*the light shines in the darkness, but the darkness has not understood it.*"

Not **understood**. That Word, which is life and light, is so utterly different from the darkness that the darkness cannot even grasp what it is about…Nor will it ever understand…and since it cannot grasp the nature of the Light, it will never be able to extinguish it. John's Prologue is the prologue to our story, our encounter with the living Word.

John got the message, but he was only one in a chain of people through the ages who have seen and recognized "the glory of the One and Only…full of grace and truth."

God of Grace and Glory, we thank you for your longing to relate to us. Open our eyes to your transforming presence among us, and the moments when the ordinary and the eternal touch. Prepare us, your children, for that day when the whole world shines with your grace and truth, made visible in the face of Jesus Christ our Lord. Amen.

Kathryn

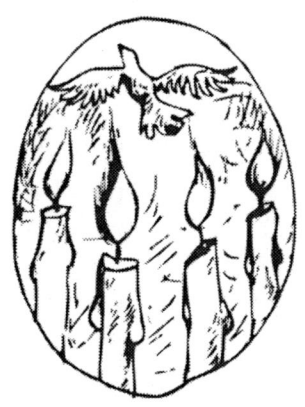

December 27

The true light, which enlightens everyone, was coming into the world. He was in the world, and the world came into being through him; yet the world did not know him. He came to what was his own, and his own people did not accept him. But to all who received him, who believed in his name, he gave power to become children of God, who were born, not of blood or of the will of the flesh or of the will of man, but of God. And the Word became flesh and lived among us, and we have seen his glory, the glory as of a father's only son, full of grace and truth.

John 1: 9 – 14 (NRSV)

Sometimes music speaks to us in a way that other things don't. I don't think there is anytime during the Church Year that this is truer than during the season of Christmas. There is just something about being at the candlelight service on Christmas Eve and singing "Silent Night, Holy Night." It has brought tears to my eyes on more than one occasion.

One of my favorite songs of all time is the Indigo Girl's "Closer to Fine." There is a line from the song that says: "Well, darkness has a hunger that's insatiable, and lightness has a call that's hard to hear." I can relate to those words. There have been times in my life when darkness seems to set the tone of my day-to-day experience. And the darkness doesn't have to be great or larger than life. Sometimes things just seem to consecutively go wrong. They may be small things, but they can munch and crunch until you feel chewed up.

When those little things begin to weigh on you it gets harder to see the lightness and hear its call. You come home from a bad day at work or you have a fight with your spouse or another bill comes along that you will have trouble paying. All those things can muffle the lightness in our lives. These are the times that I'd like to be able to throw a big switch and turn the good stuff back on and drown out the darkness.

John writes, "The true light, which enlightens everyone, was coming into the world." God likes light. It was the first thing that God made. "Let there be light," the creator said, and there was light and it was good. From the beginning of time, God wanted us to live in the light.

When John wrote his Gospel he wanted to remind us of the story of creation and that's why he begins with the beginning. "In the beginning was the Word, and the Word was with God, and the Word was God." And it's why John uses the metaphor of light when referring to the coming of Jesus. Sometimes life can be darkness that tries to swallow us whole and the words of goodness and comfort we want to hear are muffled. But Jesus is the true light and the greatest of Words and always shines through the darkness that seeks to devour us.

There is no darkness that is greater than the light of Christ that became flesh and lived among us.

God of light and life, shine in us with such abundance that we glow with your love. Shine in us with such intensity that we overflow with your goodness. Shine in us that we might spread the Word of your grace to a darkened world. Amen.

Cats

December 28

Long ago God spoke to our ancestors in many and various ways by the prophets, but in these last days he has spoken to us by a Son, whom he appointed heir of all things, through whom he also created the worlds. He is the reflection of God's glory and the exact imprint of God's very being, and he sustains all things by his powerful word. When he had made purification for sins, he sat down at the right hand of the Majesty on high, having become as much superior to angels as the name he has inherited is more excellent than theirs.
Hebrews 1:1-4 (NRSV)

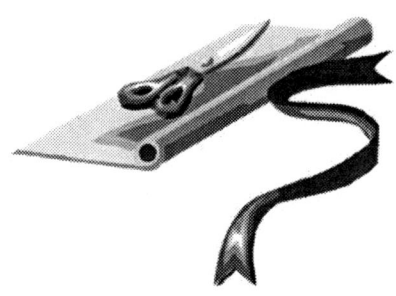

"Talk is cheap." "Actions speak louder than words." "Put your money where your mouth is." "Stick and stones may break my bones but words can never hurt me." How often do we hear these phrases during the week? How often do they come out of our own mouths, as we dissect workplace politics, or try to help our children manage playground politics? American culture thrives on action, on doing and being, on acquiring and succeeding. Sometimes we actively devalue the power of words, but other times, the importance of words fades away into the background of our fast-paced lives. I find that in my first months of ordained ministry, however, the importance of words refuses to be ignored. Whether we choose to notice or not, words are powerful, and they do matter.

In September, I returned to my seminary along with several friends and classmates to celebrate the wedding of two classmates in the school's stone chapel. We gathered in that space, made holy to us through shared memories of tears, music, words, and sacraments. We offered our gifts of singing and witness, and they stood in front of the crowd of loved ones and said, "In the name of God, I, Hope, take you Andrew, to be my husband, to have and to hold from this day forward, for better for worse, for richer for poorer, in sickness and in health, to love and to cherish, until we are parted by death. This is my solemn vow." Many things were said and done in the service, but these spoken words—shared, given, and received with love—have bound my two friends together in marriage. Certainly, words can change the direction of our lives.

Only a few short weeks earlier, I received the first early morning emergency call of my ministry. It was not from a parishioner, but from my mother. My brother had died suddenly and unexpectedly in the early morning hours. He had lived with many health problems, developmental and physical, but we were not prepared for the insulin-related heart attack that ended his life that morning. Friends and family were called, visitors came to the house, and plans for the memorial service were made. And the cards and emails began to come. Most of the notes were short and simple. "Dear Susie, There are no words. I am so sorry. Is there anything I can do? Please let me know. Peace my friend." In those sad weeks, I had no words to explain my shock or grief. How does one grieve a brother whose autism kept him in locked in his own world for his entire life? My lack of adequate words lent a kind of depth and understanding to the dark cloud of emotions. The simple words from friends, written with love and concern, made the darkness bearable and eased me through each day. Certainly, words can shine a bit of light into our darkness.

Words add to the darkness of the world when their power is wielded against our neighbors. In my own Episcopal tradition, today marks our remembrance of the Holy Innocents. Just three days after the Feast of the Nativity, the church calendar calls us to remember why we needed the child Emmanuel so desperately. I wonder how many words Herod used to order the destruction of so many children in Bethlehem. I wonder if the soldiers spoke as they murdered the young boys. I do not need to wonder if there were words to comfort the mothers, because I am sure that there were not enough words in the world to bring their boys back to life. Herod spoke a few words in a jealous rage, taking the lives of countless children and breaking the hearts of countless mothers. Certainly, words are powerful, and their power can bring great darkness to the world.

In reality, all of these words are inseparable from the actions that follow. Wedding vows are exchanged in a particular place by particular people speaking. Words of sympathy mean very little if they are not somehow shared with the receiver. Our words give birth to action and emotion, and that is their power. It is a power that can be used for good and holy purposes, or used as a means for destruction and darkness.

In the beginning was the Word, and the Word was with God, and the Word was God... and the Word became flesh and dwelt among us. At creation, God spoke and light was created. Throughout time, God has given words to us through prophets. At Christmas, the Word takes on flesh and blood, bringing light into a darkened world. The baby in the manger is the beginning of hope and the promise that light will win in the end, the superlative demonstration of Word-in-action giving birth to new life. As imitators of Jesus, we hope and pray that our words reflect the light of Christ in the world, giving birth to actions of hope and love.

In these days after Christmas, when festivities are waning and wrapping paper scatters the floor, find a quiet moment to sit still and share some of your own words in prayer. Our words of prayer may seem feeble or inadequate, but our words are answered by the Incarnate Word, who shared our human nature and sustains our being with his powerful word.

Loving God, you sent your Incarnate Word to us at Christmas to shine light in our darkness. May your light be born in our hearts again today, so that in all we say and do, your Word might be spoken and heard, to the glory and praise of Jesus Christ our Lord. Amen.

Susie Shaefer

December 29

For unto us a child is born, unto us a son is given, and the government shall be upon his shoulder, and his name shall be called Wonderful, Counsellor, The mighty God, The everlasting Father, The Prince of Peace.

Isaiah 9:6 (KJV)

December's winds cut like a wintry knife, and none so violently as the morning of the day my son was born. Back then, Advent didn't mean too much to me, as I had walked away from the church when I was about 13 and not given it much thought for the next 20 years. I went to the carols and the bells service with an infant sleeping in my lap, and it was the last time I went to church for many years.

So I can hardly blame him for his disinterest in religion. He sees the partisan rancor that calls itself "Christian" and he shakes his head. As his thirteenth birthday approached, my precociously progressive son seemed mostly interested in shaking his fist at authority and listening to loud music. I can't much blame him for that, either; I'm an old-school punk and a music critic. But I am a professional writer, so I wasn't quite as gracious when he came home not too long ago with a D in English. And because I had little faith that he would do much to change it, I prayed that God would help him connect with his studies a little better. Yes, he's read these books before, and that's why he's bored, I said. Help him to see them in a new light, so that he doesn't feel like his homework is an insult to his intelligence.

His dad, of course, grounded him and took away some of his entertainment vehicles. I talked to him about getting an A in today. Not in his class, not on his homework, but just in today. "But who gives me that grade?" my son asked. I just looked up. I know he's still getting used to mom's faith. I also know he likes what he sees, because his face lights up when we talk about getting an A in today.

We've set aside Thursday evenings to talk about school, about growing up, about anything he wants. We're already seeing results: That pesky English grade is up to a B-. Tonight, he was telling me about his trip to the National Cathedral in Washington, D.C. "It was a little religious for my tastes," he said, "but I got you a present." I closed my eyes and cupped my hands, and he poured the necklace that he had bought with his allowance into my palm.

My son, o he of little faith, had gotten me exactly what I wanted for my birthday: a small Jerusalem cross. He didn't know why he had picked it out; it suited his budget, and it appealed to him. He had no idea that I had been hoping to run across something exactly like this, and that I expected it would come from my parents or godparents as a token of congratulations for having discerned something resembling a call—a thing I am still working on, still listening for, and still unsure of.

But God spoke through my son, today, as he did with his son. Sometimes we are hard-pressed to listen for God, much less listen to him, but I think we both heard him today. As we reflect on the gifts we are given this holiday season, let us remember that there is no gift greater than love, the same love God had to give his son to us.

Heavenly Father, we thank you for your love and for sending us the people in our lives who love us as you do. Help us to remember those who depend on us and upon whom we depend, and to acknowledge the ways in which they reveal your grace. Bring healing to broken hearts, renewal to shaken faith, and peace to our fragile earth, for the love of your son, our Savior, Wonderful Counsellor, Jesus Christ. Amen.

Gallycat

December 30

*O sing to the Lord a new song,
for he has done marvelous things.
His right hand and his holy arm have gotten him victory.
Make a joyful noise to the Lord, all the earth;
Break forth into joyous song and sing praises.
Sing praises to the Lord with the lyre,
with the lyre and the sound of melody.
With trumpets and the sound of the horn
make a joyful noise before the King, the Lord.
Let the sea roar, and all that fills it;
the world and those who live in it.
Let the floods clap their hands;
let the hills sing together for joy
At the presence of the Lord,
for he is coming to judge the earth.
He will judge the world with righteousness,
and the peoples with equity.*

Psalm 98:1, 4-9 (NRSV)

In the middle of writing this devotional the first time, a very disturbing thing happened in my life: my house ceased to have running water. Like most modern conveniences, I never noticed how dependent I am upon running water until I didn't have it. For five days I felt half dead: grimy, weary, and just plain out of sync with everything and everyone around me. I'm sure I was absolutely insufferable to all those subjected to my presence. I certainly couldn't be expected to write a cheerful devotional entry about making joyful noise to the Lord. I was entirely too cranky to sing to the Lord a new song, or even an old song, while I was trying to figure out how to bathe effectively with bottled water.

It's funny how relatively minor inconveniences can make us see the whole world as a gritty, greasy, grotesque mess. The slightest glitch in our plans, the smallest break in our established routine, can render us almost incapable of seeing anything good about life – or even about God. We might cry out to God from our dark places, but singing praise often seems beyond us when things are going wrong.

On my fifth day without running water, I returned home late one night. I had heard a rumor that a real, live, professional plumber had finally been sent to the parsonage to check out the situation. I have to admit that my reaction had been a rather sarcastic, "Dare to dream!" Nonetheless, I had just enough hope to make me run up the stairs and check the bathtub faucet. A sad little sputter, a few small spurts, an alarming burst of air, and then…actual running water.

Honestly, I don't think I have ever been so utterly joyful and thankful as I was in that moment. I wanted to jump up and down, twirl, throw my hands in the air, and sing a few rounds of "The Hallelujah Chorus." So I did. And then I fell onto my knees and thrust my hands into the flowing stream of water and thanked God. In the scheme of things, I'm sure a little running water isn't really that big of a deal, but I swear, in that moment, even the water itself applauded wildly.

Running water is in our culture a little thing, so minor it seems almost silly to write about it. It's an ordinary thing, an expected thing, something we take for granted, something barely worth mentioning. But if it's the little obstacles and the minor interruptions that so often cause our emotional collapse, why shouldn't it be all the more true that it's the little joys that remind us of the beauty of this world and the glory of its Creator? I don't seem to need a tragedy to sink into despondency, which makes me all the more glad that I don't need a miracle to cause me to break into joyous song.

Miracles happen in this world, I know. Sometimes people mysteriously survive disasters and suddenly recover from horrible illnesses. Sometimes money and food arrive at just the right time, against all odds. More often, though, what we get is the little, ordinary things: the perfect sunrise over the ocean, the sparkling beauty of the first snowfall of winter, the simple joy of a cup of great coffee, the warm melting sweetness of a chocolate-chip cookie just out of the oven, the much-needed embrace of a friend, the cool relief of running water. We might wish for big miracles, dramatic signs of God's presence and help in our lives, but most of the time, God chooses to work in and through the small things. From these seemingly ordinary events, God pieces together a world that, from time to time, causes us to sing a new song to the Lord.

The event we celebrate at Christmas is no exception. Many years ago, God chose to do the greatest work of all, through something that happens every day. A baby was born. Of course, this baby was a miracle to his parents, as babies almost always are, but on the whole, he probably seemed a perfectly ordinary child. The birth of a baby is, in the great scheme of things, a little event, a normal occurrence. Yet, through this tiny baby, God was ushering into the world a great miracle: the very incarnation of God in human flesh.

Later it would be said about this child that if his disciples did not lift their voices, even the rocks would shout for joy at his coming. I would wager that perhaps the seas and the hills might also join in the chorus, and us along with them, "at the presence of the Lord, for he is coming to judge the earth. He will judge the world with righteousness, and the peoples with equity." Make a joyful noise to the Lord, all the earth, for Christ the Savior is born.

Lord of all things great and small, we sing to you a new song, for you have done marvelous things. With the seas and the floods and all of your worshippers, we join in joyful chorus of praise sung by all the earth in celebration of birth of our savior, Jesus Christ. We thank you for the ways that you come to us in the small and ordinary things, just as you came for us in the small and ordinary human body of a baby. Give us eyes to appreciate the many ways you appear to us, whether subtle or dramatic, and voices to raise in songs of praise for the coming of our Lord. Amen.

Rev. Stacey

December 31

> *I'm tired of all this— so tired. My bed*
> *has been floating forty days and nights*
> *On the flood of my tears.*
> *My mattress is soaked, soggy with tears.*
> *The sockets of my eyes are black holes;*
> *nearly blind, I squint and grope.*
>
> **Psalm 6:6-8 (*The Message*)**

What are you doing New Year's Eve?

For many people it's just a social question. They might be going out with friends, or planning a quiet night "in" for two. Some friends of ours have a game night at home with their four children and a number of their young friends. It is such a happy, established family ritual that even as the older children went off to college and reached their twenties, they continued to bring friends home for the evening.

But I can remember some New Year's Eves with the mood of Psalm 6. In this lament, the psalmist cries out for God to stop picking on him. "O, Lord—how long?" she cries.

Now, things weren't actually worse on New Year's Eve. Life was essentially the same as it had been the day before and would be the day after. But the combination of the dried-out Christmas tree, the social and cultural expectations and the exceedingly slow return of light can add up to a painful evening for a person who feels lonely. The hours and minutes counting down toward minute can feel interminable. Surely everyone else is having fun?

I remember a sad New Year's Eve. It was the end of a year when I had been divorced, sold my house, moved my children into interim housing, tried to go back to school and finally lost my father very suddenly. At New Year's the children and I were at my dad's house, beginning the work of sorting out and packing up necessary for selling the house. When we arrived there, after a long journey by airplane and car, the furnace wasn't working. The weather was dark. The house seemed seized by gloom; my eyes were dim; my heart was heavy. We spent New Year's Eve rattling around the enormous house trying to stay warm. The usual components of that night, the champagne, the parties, the kiss—these were as distant as they had ever been. I was bone tired and heart lonely.

O, Lord—how long?

A psalm is more than a poem or a prayer. It is a ritual, a way of working through the problem. Walter Breuggemann says a psalm of lament is a "song of disarray." Whether the illness in Psalm 6 is a cancer of the body or a depression of the soul or an injustice within the community, the psalmist is desperate. But this suffering person knows what to do. This suffering person brings his worry, her sorrow, their mistreatment to God.

Our lamenting is a crucial part of our healing.

O, Lord—how long?

Some scholars will tell you that the gap in that phrase reflects a lost piece of text, but I don't believe it. The empty space describes the distance we feel when we are afraid God doesn't care about us. We want to know how much longer our suffering will go on, yes, but we also want to know where God is!!!

We celebrate a New Year when we do because ten days after the shortest day there is finally a convincing amount of light returning. The days will lengthen. The night will decrease.

> *Get out of here, you Devil's crew:*
> *at last God has heard my sobs.*
> *My requests have all been granted,*
> *my prayers are answered.*
>
> **Psalm 6:8-9 (*The Message*)**

It may be that the "devil's crew," the enemies named, were real people for some petitioners who prayed this psalm. But when God's presence is the question, the demons are usually our own. God is there all along, whether it is a long night, a lonely evening or an unbearable day. God is there all along, when our complaints overwhelm our reason, our injuries hobble us, or our tears threaten to wash us away. God is there. The work of the psalm is to move us through the dark places and into a renewed awareness of God's presence. We are never alone. God is there all along.

Loving God, on dark and lonely nights, we cry out to you: O Lord—how long? Help us to find you again, we pray. Amen.

Songbird

January 1

I will greatly rejoice in the LORD, my whole being shall exult in my God; for he has clothed me with the garments of salvation, he has covered me with the robe of righteousness, as a bridegroom decks himself with a garland, and as a bride adorns herself with her jewels. For as the earth brings forth its shoots, and as a garden causes what is sown in it to spring up, so the Lord GOD will cause righteousness and praise to spring up before all the nations.

For Zion's sake I will not keep silent, and for Jerusalem's sake I will not rest, until her vindication shines out like the dawn, and her salvation like a burning torch. The nations shall see your vindication, and all the kings your glory; and you shall be called by a new name that the mouth of the LORD will give. You shall be a crown of beauty in the hand of the LORD, and a royal diadem in the hand of your God. You shall no more be termed Forsaken, and your land shall no more be termed Desolate; but you shall be called My Delight Is in Her, and your land Married; for the LORD delights in you, and your land shall be married. For as a young man marries a young woman, so shall your builder marry you, and as the bridegroom rejoices over the bride, so shall your God rejoice over you.

Isaiah 61:10-62:5 (NRSV)

It's a standard plot line of film and television comedies, from *Muriel's Wedding* to *Everybody Loves Raymond* —the woman who makes her wedding day her primary concern in life, even more so than her relationship with her loved one, who in these stories often seems to be a prop rather than a partner to the wedding-obsessed fiancée. And while women are seen in our culture as being more concerned than men about having a Big Day, it's probably safe to say that for many men their wedding day feels like a vindication of their manhood, a definitive crossing over the threshold into adulthood, into "real" life.

The author of Isaiah 61-62 uses the imagery of a wedding to describe a restored Jerusalem's relationship with God. Zion is described as being clothed in salvation and righteousness like a bride or bridegroom adorned for the wedding ceremony; Zion is given a new name and status, like a bride; Zion is told that God will rejoice in her, will delight in her.

As I read and re-read this text, a question persistently inserted itself into my meditations: *What happens when the honeymoon is over?*

Many of us, just days after joyously celebrating our Lord's arrival—the extraordinary marriage of God and humanity in the person of Jesus—are suffering from post-Christmas letdown. This is especially true in a consumer culture where, contrary to the rhythms of the Church year, the "Christmas season" begins as soon as the back-to-school sales end (if not sooner) and is over in many cases by Christmas afternoon, when some of us are already dragging our Christmas trees to the curb. Instead of nurturing Jesus anew in our hearts, we often find ourselves, figuratively speaking, wrapping the Baby up in tissue paper with the rest of our *creche* and putting him away for another year.

"Christ our Savior is born," we sing. Christmas has come and gone. The party's over, so to speak. Now what?

I think the answer lies in the response that one of my campus pastors used to give to antagonistic campus evangelists who would try to get him entangled in arguments over whether or not he or the rest of us in our church were "saved." He used to respond, "Saved *for what?*"

The message of the prophet, in the voice of the Servant, is a message of hope, but also of justice, and of expanding the Reign of God beyond the faith community, to "all the nations." The Servant, in these texts, gives Israel a job to do: to be "priests of the Lord" and "ministers of our God."

In one of our family albums there's a picture of one of my female ancestors in her wedding outfit—a long white veil drifting over a dark, everyday dress. I remember, when I was younger, asking about this, and being told that, back in the 19th century, most brides could not afford a special wedding dress; their dress had to serve double duty as a utilitarian article of clothing. It was a visual reminder that, indeed, real life was waiting after the "I do's."

How do we keep Christmas well, as Dickens put it, after the holiday hoopla, when the rest of the culture seems to have already forgotten the miracle of God-with-us and is rushing headlong toward the secular concerns of the New Year? By attending to the question, "Saved for what?" The best way to honor the coming of the Lord Jesus into our midst is to carry him into the situations that present themselves in our lives: works of compassion; works of justice; words of grace; telling the Story as it has been told to us and lived into us.

It's at this time of year that we hear about the Magi presenting the young Jesus with gifts of gold, frankincense and myrrh. The best gift we can give him is… ourselves; our time, our talents, our possessions, given for the benefit of our neighbors near and far, to his glory.

Christianity is, above all things, a *relational* faith. Just as marriage is a relationship, not an event, our individual and corporate relationship with Christ is a relationship: *I was saved; I am being saved; I will be saved.* Christ loves us; redeems us; calls us into relationship. We in turn respond to this love and grace by sharing that love and grace with others; that is one of the things that keeps the spark in our relationship with Christ. We're adorned like brides and bridegrooms; but like our practical ancestors, God also dresses us in clothes ready for work in the world, ready for living Christ into it. That is the journey, the adventure, of our lives with and in God, as God in Christ says, "I do" to us.

Gracious and loving God, we thank and praise you for the gift of yourself in the person of Jesus Christ. We thank you for giving us a "new name," a new relationship with you, and a new job of ministering to the world on your behalf. Help us to live your righteousness, and sing your praise, into our world. We pray this in the name of Jesus Christ, who lives and reigns with you and the Holy Spirit, one God, now and forever. Amen.

Lutheranchik

January 2

Praise the LORD from the heavens! Praise him in the heights above. Praise him, all his angels of his; praise him, all his heavenly hosts! Praise him, sun and moon: praise him, all you shining stars. Praise him, you highest heavens, and you waters above the skies. Let them praise the name of the LORD, for he commanded, and they were created...

Psalm 148 (NIV)

Music has always been my major form of worship. I grew up in a family that took guitar lessons together and played in the Folk Mass when it began in our church in the 1970s. My mother ran a church group for pre-adolescent girls and we put on Christian musicals. Though I was a girl, I played King Nebuchadnezzar and King Naaman –it's good to be tall!

My love for music extended into school choir. My two last summers in high school, I attended choir camp at a small university in the northern part of my state. About six hundred kids from all over Texas we spent about a week in intensive study of the music for the State Choir auditions that would be held in the fall. I hasten to add that I never *made* State choir—or Region, or even District! I can usually carry a tune, but I am very much a garden-variety singer. I was, however, devoted to the choir director and the program at my school.

The last year of camp was fantastic. My friends and I said afterward that working with the chief clinician was "a musical experience." There were several pieces, including a marvelous setting of Psalm 148 by John Rutter. It's a sweeping festival anthem for double choir and orchestra, and the text is incomparable. The psalmist calls upon "everything that hath breath (to) praise the Lord!" including *great sea creatures and all deeps, young men and maidens, old men and children,* and also some things that do <u>not</u> have breath: *fire and hail, snow and vapor, wind and storm.* I loved learning that piece and the others. On the last day of camp, we performed all of the music we had learned for a taped session.

There was so much electricity in the room when we were performing the Rutter *Psalm 148*—my hair was standing up! The clinician cut off the choir's final note, and the pianist thundered the final chords. Then the room erupted in a wave of sound—applause, shrieks, whoops. I had tears in my eyes. Whenever I listen to that tape (which I have over and over through the years), I have the same reaction. It has actually brought me through some fairly dark times.

When I was growing up, my parents had always been active in the church, so I was too (not having a choice). They were careful to raise us up "in the way we should go, so that when we were old we should not depart from it" (Proverbs 22:6). So I know it was a huge disappointment to them when, as I began college, I fell away from the Church. I think I needed some time to figure out who I was, on my own, and what my relationship with God was. I never thought there might not be a God, but I was rather disappointed in the ways I felt he or she was letting the world down, and the way that the Episcopal Church was, too. (Does this sound familiar?) I tried various types of churches, but I never felt afterward that I had truly worshipped. I was studying the Great Enlightenment of the Eighteenth Century, but in truth I was wandering in the dark.

One of the things that I held onto throughout my unchurched years was that recording of Psalm 148. I played it when I was particularly happy or sad. My roommates got very tired of hearing it! But the idea of the whole world praising the Lord, *flying birds and creeping things, princes and all rulers of the world*, made me feel better. Looking back, I believe that I was waiting and hoping at some point to again feel comfortable within my Episcopal upbringing.

I had to spend about eight years alone in the darkness, and be brought extra-low by addiction and a bad relationship, before I stumbled back to St. Francis, the small Episcopal congregation that had been waiting for me all along. I was loved and held, and my wounds were bound up; there was wonderful worship and music and community. We praised the Lord in every way: traditional hymns, contemporary worship music; liturgical dance; and with instruments as varied as the piano, guitar, bodhran (a Celtic drum), maracas and harmonica.

I had thought that perhaps after such a long absence, God and his Church would not take me back. Was I ever wrong! When I finally let go of my pride and walked back into the light, I realized that the song of praise had never stopped and that I had always been part of it.

Lord Jesus, help us to share with others the accepting love you show us. Remind us that you are big enough to deal with our doubts, and that you and your Father are always waiting for us to join the song of praise again if we should stray.

Mary Beth/Terrapin Station

January 3

But when the time had fully come, God sent his Son, born of a woman, born under law, to redeem those under law, that we might receive the full rights of sons. Because you are sons, God sent the Spirit of his Son into our hearts, the Spirit who calls out, 'Abba, Father.' So you are no longer a slave, but a son; and since you are a son, God has made you also an heir.

Matthew 2:4-7 (NIV)

So much of the Bible is lost in translation. I'm not a Greek scholar but passages like this one make me wish I were. In the world in which we live, it's easy for women to feel overlooked and undervalued. I know I sometimes do. That can cause us to look at passages like today's and be put off because it doesn't use gender inclusive language like children or at least sons *and* daughters. We can feel excluded, but we shouldn't because that isn't the spirit of the passage at all.

This passage is all about God's love. But to understand it we do need to get beyond the language. Paul uses almost the same words in Romans 8:14-17: *Those of you who are led by the Spirit of God are sons of God. For you did not receive a spirit that makes you a slave again to fear, but you received the Spirit of sonship. And by him we cry "Abba Father" ... Now if we are God's children, then we are heirs— heirs of God and co-heirs with Christ.* Yes Paul does use the word son, and to add the word daughter to it, while acceptable, is actually rather misleading. The underlying idea here I think is *adoption.*

Almost certainly some of you are adopted. I'm not, but a couple of my friends are, while others I know have adopted children of their own. We in the west are used to children being adopted, and it's such a wonderful gift to give to a child who, for whatever reason, cannot live with his or her biological parents. Adoption was common among the Greeks and the Romans too, and it was a legal transaction whereby the adopted child was given all the privileges of a natural child, including inheritance rights. It could never be revoked.

Paul tells us that we are adopted by God. Our Heavenly Father has given each of us—whatever our gender—the status of son and heir. We have been made co-heirs with Christ. And that status can never be revoked. Let that sink in for a minute: It means that Father God loves us as much as he loves Jesus Christ and nothing we do, or fail to do, can nullify our adoption. We—males and females—are God's heirs, because we are redeemed by Jesus' blood. It's an amazing promise!

Only ten days ago we celebrated Jesus' birth. Paul tells us that Jesus was "born of a woman, born under law, to redeem those under law, that we might receive the full rights of sons." The basis for the incarnation, the crucifixion and resurrection was, and is, God's love for us. Scripture tells us that we cannot possibly know the depth of God's love, (Eph 3:14-19) but John 3:16 (probably the most well know Bible verse of all) gives us a glimpse: *"For God so loved the world that he gave his one and only Son, that whoever believes in him shall not perish but have eternal life."*

God's love makes the difference in our lives. Each of us has a unique and amazing story to tell. And tell it we should. I love the story of the lost son in Luke 15. There are three people in the story; sometimes I identify with the father or the younger son, but mostly I've identified with the older brother. He, like me, strived for attention, feared rejection and tried to earn love and recognition. Yet when his renegade brother came home, he refused to celebrate with his father. I was just like that!

One day my life changed. I had prayed that God would make me a better person when suddenly I realized God loved me for who I was, no matter what. From then on his love could flow into my life and free me to see myself through his eyes. I was, and am, loved, cherished and precious, worth sending his son for. And so are you, because that is how God sees each and every one of us.

God's love can and often does come to us through another person. Church, dear friends, is not the worship or the liturgy, it's not the Eucharist or the sermon, it's not even the Scriptures or the prayers, wonderful though all these are; church is letting His love run through us, until it touches the lives of others, so that they too can cry out "Abba, Daddy, Papa, Pop: I am so loved by You."

Almighty God, you know our hearts and our minds, our desires and hopes, our faults and failings, yet when we dare to look into your eyes, we see your love reflected back. Your gaze restores us and heals us, and we know that we are so loved and cherished. We thank you that we are your children, loved as much as Jesus. You are a good Father. Help us to bathe in the security of that relationship. And as we are transformed by your love, help us share it with those we meet.

Lorna

January 4

After eight days had passed, it was time to circumcise the child; and he was called Jesus, the name given by the angel before he was conceived in the womb. When the time came for their purification according to the law of Moses, they brought him up to Jerusalem to present him to the Lord (as it is written in the law of the Lord, 'Every firstborn male shall be designated as holy to the Lord'), and they offered a sacrifice according to what is stated in the law of the Lord, 'a pair of turtle-doves or two young pigeons.'

Now there was a man in Jerusalem whose name was Simeon; this man was righteous and devout, looking forward to the consolation of Israel, and the Holy Spirit rested on him. It had been revealed to him by the Holy Spirit that he would not see death before he had seen the Lord's Messiah

There was also a prophet, Anna the daughter of Phanuel, of the tribe of Asher. She was of a great age, having lived with her husband for seven years after her marriage, then as a widow to the age of eighty-four. She never left the temple but worshipped there with fasting and prayer night and day. At that moment she came, and began to praise God and to speak about the child to all who were looking for the redemption of Jerusalem.

When they had finished everything required by the law of the Lord, they returned to Galilee, to their own town of Nazareth. The child grew and became strong, filled with wisdom; and the favor of God was upon him.

Luke 2: 21-26,36–40 (NRSV)

When Jesus was just a little over a week old, Mary and Joseph took him to the temple to be dedicated to God. While the family was in the temple, they met two very interesting and spiritual people…Simeon and Anna.

Simeon was a dedicated religious man, one who had looked and looked for the Messiah. Perhaps that became his lifetime interest—even his obsession. He was one of the first people to see Jesus after his birth. And not only did Simeon get to see the baby, he had the privilege of holding him. His lifetime of dedication had paid off… he received the gift of seeing God's gift to the world.

Simeon wasn't the only one who saw the baby Jesus. Anna was a woman who most likely had much pain in her life. For 84 years she had been a widow, alone after just seven years of marriage. We're told that she too was very dedicated to God… staying at the temple day and night. She was a prophetess, devout in praying to and praising God in spite of the pain and sorrow that undoubtedly filled her heart and her life. As she was about her daily practice of praying and fasting, she became aware that something was different in the temple. Anna heard the excitement and Simeon's words and when she did, she broke into heartfelt, joyful praise. She knew that this child that she was singing over was the one she had been waiting for… the one who would save the people of Israel.

Through their dedication, Anna and Simeon can teach each of us something very valuable. Simeon, because he had heard about the promise of the Messiah, had lived in hopeful expectation that one day he would witness the Messiah in his midst. He would awaken in anticipation each day that this day could be the one where his life would be made complete. Following guidance of the Spirit, Simeon entered the temple that day hoping that this day would be different, more extraordinary than the days before, and it was. Simeon, because of his faith and his dedication to the promises of God made through the prophets, was given the opportunity to have this close encounter with the Savior of the world.

Anna, this widow that was so dedicated to God that she stayed in the temple day and night, was able to see the baby that would grow into the greatest man to ever walk the face of the earth. It would have been understandable if Anna had been resentful toward God because of the sorrow that was a part of her life. But instead of being bitter, Anna made it her tradition to remain in the house of God and worship there. Through her fasting, her prayers and her dedication to God, Anna was also given the gift of being one of the first people to see the Messiah.

What can we learn from these two devoted people who lived so long ago? Dedication. Both Anna and Simeon were dedicated to

God. They lived a life of dedication in which each was searching... looking for the promises of God to be fulfilled. They both expected to see the Messiah in their lifetimes, and because of their faith, they were blessed with the opportunity to see Jesus face to face. Had they not been looking for the Messiah in their midst, I wonder if they would have been as blessed.

Faith calls us to be just that... faithful. We are called to believe in the scriptures and what they say. We are called to trust in God to be a faithful God in spite of the circumstances that we may be facing at the time. Anna and Simeon were blessed that day because they had faith and they faithfully looked for God to fulfill God's promises. If they woke up that day and thought, "I doubt that anything extraordinary will happen," they would have missed out on a once in a lifetime event.

Each day, we are encouraged by the examples of Simeon and Anna to wake up with expectation. What would each day look like if we expected to see God in our midst? What would each day look like if, in spite of the events in our lives, we woke up each day with the true joy and love of God in our hearts? Love and joy that we are ready and willing to share with all those who come into our midst.

As this new year is beginning, we are challenged by the example of these two who were so faithful, to dedicate ourselves. We are encouraged to be in prayer every day and to participate in the spiritual disciplines like fasting. We are encouraged to allow the Holy Spirit to guide us in the things that we do. And we are encouraged to trust in God to fulfill God's promises in our midst, because above all else, God is faithful. When we devote our lives to the perpetual worship of God, expecting to see miracles, we can witness extraordinary things. And by living faithfully, we will be most attuned to see Christ in our midst.

Lord, With our own eyes we have seen your salvation; we know him and thank you that he is now out in the open for everyone to see: he is a God-revealing light to us all, and He reveals the wonder of glory for your people . Keep us faithful to your light, help us to faithful as your servants Anna and Simeon. Keep us in the reassurance that one day we will indeed see you face to face. In the name of your Son, Amen.

Smallest Angel

January 5

In those days Jesus came from Nazareth of Galilee and was baptized by John in the Jordan. And just as he was coming up out of the water, he saw the heavens torn apart and the Spirit descending like a dove on him. And a voice came from heaven, 'You are my Son, the Beloved; with you I am well pleased.'

Mark 1: 9-11 (NRSV)

I was sixteen years old when I was baptized and confirmed in the household and family of God, within the United Church of Canada. Our denomination practices infant baptism, but I was a latecomer to the church and so received the "package deal" of combined baptism and adult confirmation. I was raised in a loving home surrounded by people who lived every essential teaching of the Christian faith, but until my sixteenth year, I had not set foot in a church.

When I was a young child, we started our school day by singing "Jesus Loves Me" followed by our national anthem, "O Canada." Then we said The Lord's Prayer. For an unchurched child, I must say, it was all very confusing. At one point, I was certain that Jesus lived on Parliament Hill, running the country in a very loving way!

In my teens I became curious about faith and went with my friend to a Good Friday vigil. My introduction to church was a solid three hours of reflection on the suffering of Christ, followed by trumpets and joy two days later. After that, I never looked back. My life was changed. A year after that first Easter celebration, I was baptized. My future father-in-law was the presiding clergy. It was a beautiful, Spirit-filled moment.

I remember the awesome feeling of being linked irreversibly to the historic practice of baptism through the ages. I remember envisioning John as he humbly baptized the One he knew to be the Messiah. I wondered if John's hands were shaking as he took hold of Jesus and performed the baptism. I thought about how full his heart must have been. I tried to imagine all that Jesus experienced that day and the new life that began for him as he emerged from the water.

I felt in that moment as if a fine, barely discernable thread connected me to the whole communion of saints, past and present, who proclaim the gospel of Christ. The air seemed to reverberate with the playful dancing of the Spirit, and I was awestruck.

An elderly woman in the congregation took me under her wing. She liked to have a tea cup (never a mug!) of hot water after worship, and she cleverly arranged for me to get it from the kitchen. On those Sundays when my adolescent nature invited me to sleep in, I would think my frail, smiling friend waiting at church for me to come and see her. She will never know the power of those cups of water, or the way her smile told me I was a part of something wonderful.

Over the years, I've had the usual roller coaster ride of joy and disillusionment with this mysterious entity we know as Church. The politics can make my head spin, but there are also moments of grace and simple beauty that take me back to my baptism and that feeling of awe and wonder. Such moments, those life-changing moments of clarity and faith, are the true power of Christ's church. Take away all the window dressing – all the stained glass and pretty wood and cathedral grandeur, all the denominational posturing and politics – take that away, and you are left with two men standing in a muddy river listening to the word of God saying, *"You are my Son, the Beloved."*

The baptism of Jesus reminds me that we are called to *unity* in Christ, not to endless divisions based on liturgical and dogmatic minutiae. We are invited to remember where it all started. In humility, we stand on the shores of the Jordan River and accept the gift of Jesus' baptism as a gift that all of us share, together.

If true unity in the body of Christ is the goal, we, as the Church, will have to make some serious changes. Like any worthwhile venture, doing so comes with an element of risk and uncertainty. Transforming Christ's church will be no small task. We may have to wash away the power plays and political dynamics that have hindered Christ's church for so long. We may have to wash away attachments to what *was* if those things are blurring our vision of what *can be*. We may need to die to a whole lot of things before we can really live again – this time in unity.

As a church, we may need a baptism by fire to take us back to the pure simplicity of that day in the river. Perhaps then, by grace, unfettered by division and hurt, we will hear again the words of the Holy saying, "*…in you I am well pleased.*"

Loving and Most Gracious God, dance in our midst, we pray. Remind us that we are linked to You and to one another by the Spirit and by our baptism. Guide us in wisdom and grace as we seek to love and serve you, this day and every day, in Jesus' name. Amen.

Inner Dorothy

January 6

Arise, shine; for your light has come, and the glory of the LORD has risen upon you. For darkness shall cover the earth, and thick darkness the peoples; but the LORD will arise upon you, and his glory will appear over you. Nations shall come to your light, and kings to the brightness of your dawn. Lift up your eyes and look around; they all gather together, they come to you; your sons shall come from far away, and your daughters shall be carried on their nurses' arms. Then you shall see and be radiant; your heart shall thrill and rejoice, because the abundance of the sea shall be brought to you, the wealth of the nations shall come to you.
Isaiah 60:1-5 (NRSV)

It was the year that my son Phil, who has autism, was just turning four. He was disruptive at just about every event I attempted to include him in, and I was frustrated. Just the week before, he had rolled in the mud at the Easter Egg hunt. He'd gotten mud all over the expensive Easter clothes of any of the kids who attempted to help the "poor autistic boy" find the eggs. (His issue was that eggs are not supposed to be in the grass, nor are they supposed to be different colors, and he was upset that anyone would do that to eggs. A couple of years later, it would be very humorous to him, but that year it sent him into a panic.) We couldn't go anyplace or do anything!

He had been causing disruptions in worship. We were still dealing with the whole diagnosis nightmare and trying to figure out how to live with a child who had aggressive panic attacks and no language, while attempting to remain within, and include him in, whatever communities we could possibly relate to. It wasn't easy. Sometimes he caused big honking disruptions before we could get him out of there. Living with him was one big disruption and frustration for everyone around him.

The day before Easter, we received an anonymous letter from someone in the church. It said that Phil was disruptive in church and was ruining the experience of the worship of God for everyone in the congregation. It was unsigned, but claimed to be from a number of folks who were asking if we would please sit in the back row and remove the child sooner, or better yet, not even attend worship with that child. The letter was just another devastating reminder that our lives were changing in ways that felt really out of control to me. Like I didn't know he was disruptive, and I wasn't doing everything I could possibly think of?

On Easter Day, I brought Phil to church. We did not go into the sanctuary as a family. My eight-year-old daughter and my husband were participating in the music in worship. I took my son out to the swing set just outside the sanctuary. As the worship service began, I stood there, pushing him on the swing, tears in my eyes, feeling sorry for "us," angry with Phil, with "anonymous," with the congregation, with the world, and with God, in that daze I lived within during those years. Phil began to swing. In the rhythm of that swinging, he sang, forcefully, to the rhythm of his swinging, one phrase, over and over again. He couldn't talk, but he has good rhythm and pitch, and eventually I figured out what song it was. "I duh duh-duh… I duh duh-duh… I am the church… I am the church!" I was looking for "it," grabbing for "it," and hoping for "it," and there It was all the time, in ways I'd never imagined "it." It wasn't what I'd wanted or hoped for, but there It was—God— Christ—the Church. "I am the church!"

My son taught me a lot that day, about a lot of things, though I haven't a clue how much of it he understood himself. I'm still learning about what it means that someone like him— disruptive, difficult, and dirty—IS the church. I keep thinking I've found where to look for God and where to look for Church, and it always ends up appearing where I least expect.

Epiphany: The words of the prophets really can be written on the "subway walls and tenement halls." And the moment I become certain I will find them even there, they are gone, to another country, awaiting the right moment to return. "Open our eyes…"

Dearest Lord, thank you that in your wisdom you see that we are the church together — all that follow Jesus, all around the world. Open our eyes so that we see Jesus all around us. We see the baby in the manger, we see the man on the cross. We see Jesus in the eyes of the homeless man in the streets and hear his voice in the song of small boys who can only whisper his words into the sound of silence.

Jenee from Textweek

January 7

John the baptizer appeared in the wilderness, proclaiming a baptism of repentance for the forgiveness of sins. And people from the whole Judean countryside and all the people of Jerusalem were going out to him, and were baptized by him in the river Jordan, confessing their sins. Now John was clothed with camel's hair, with a leather belt around his waist, and he ate locusts and wild honey. He proclaimed, 'The one who is more powerful than I is coming after me; I am not worthy to stoop down and untie the thong of his sandals. I have baptized you with water; but he will baptize you with the Holy Spirit.'

In those days Jesus came from Nazareth of Galilee and was baptized by John in the Jordan. And just as he was coming up out of the water, he saw the heavens torn apart and the Spirit descending like a dove on him. And a voice came from heaven, 'You are my Son, the Beloved; with you I am well pleased.'

Mark 1:4-11 (NRSV)

After a month of Advent and Christmas and a day after Epiphany, it seems odd to be reading Mark's gospel today...particularly when the first part of today's Gospel lesson was part of the Advent texts just about a month ago. This passage is the first appearance of Jesus Christ in Mark's gospel...For Mark there are no angels, no shepherds, no magi, no Mary, no Joseph.

Like the writer of Genesis, whose work he seems to know rather well, Mark begins with water. He adds a well-tanned, wild-eyed prophet named John standing waist deep in the Jordan, bending over this man who has come all the way from Galilee, baptizing him. The man's face breaks the surface of the water. He rises, water cascading off his beard and hair, and as he does, the man—Jesus—sees the heavens open, and the same Spirit who brooded over the face of the waters in Genesis descends upon him like a dove...and just as in Genesis, God speaks a word of satisfied pleasure...Instead of "it is Good" God says... "You are my Son, the Beloved; with you I am well pleased."

For Mark, the full identity of Jesus is revealed in this moment. Mark has no need for the accoutrements of the Season. He has this water, the heavens opening, this Spirit, this voice from heaven. Together they begin the story— the story of God's engagement with the world, or rather, the story of God's re-engagement with the world in the life, death, and resurrection of Jesus of Nazareth.

If you look at it as Biblical literature it is amazing—Mark has borrowed language and imagery from throughout the Old Testament. In addition to the allusions to Genesis...there are so many more... "You are my son" which God speaks in Psalm 2...the heavens opening from Isaiah and Ezekiel...the descent of the spirit...again from Isaiah. But this isn't just a beautiful piece of literature....It is one writer's attempt to use language and symbols that would be familiar to his readers to say "Pay attention...this man is special...God is doing a new and prophetic and wonderful thing here!" He does this to introduce us to the Son of God...by sharing an intimate encounter between a young man and a loving heavenly parent.

Did you notice...only Jesus hears God's message and only Jesus sees the Spirit descending...and this is unique to Mark's gospel. The baptism of Jesus is one of the few events in the life and ministry of Jesus that is set out in all four gospels. But over in Matthew...everyone sees and God doesn't say "you are my Son;" God announces... "This is my Son." In Luke, God says "you" but all can see the dove. In John, the voice and spirit are at least visible to John the Baptist.

And which is more consistent with what we know of God speaking to God's children? Still I don't know about you, but this whole idea of God speaking to Jesus makes me a little uncomfortable. I tend to be skeptical about those who claim to have heard a word from God. From Oral Roberts' "Give me 10 million dollars or I'm dead" to the seminarian who is so sure of her calling that she encountered it as an actual voice, I'm just a little nervous with God speaking out loud to someone, even to Jesus.

But there they are, parent and child, whispering words of love and family and acceptance. Jesus hears the voice of God and receives a wonderful gift, a sense of affirmation and identity that begin his ministry. From the banks of the Jordan he will go to the wilderness to pray and fast...he will be tested...and he will begin his public ministry. Jesus hears these words of God and they are enough…these powerful words sustain him in the trials that lay ahead…all the way to a cross and an empty tomb.

And if we are really listening, can't we have some idea of what Mark is talking about? Tomorrow we are called to remember our baptisms and the baptisms of our children, and of all God's children, and isn't that one of the reasons why we baptize? That sign and seal of God in Christ calling out, sometimes in a loud voice that all can hear and sometimes in a quiet voice that only we can hear, "You are my child…You are my daughter, my beloved…in you I am well pleased." Surely, if we can but live as though those words are true, won't they be enough for us too?

Whispering Parent, we strain to hear your words of love above the din of everyday concerns, the clanging cymbals of culture and clan, the roar of war and dehumanizing injustice. Speak your words of affirmation again, loud and strong, to remind us that we are your children, sisters and brothers with Christ and with one another. Remind us that your love is steadfast, unadorned, and true. Open us to the truth of your transforming love, love enough for today and for our every tomorrow. Amen.

ChicagoRev/NotShyChiRev

January 8

John the baptizer appeared in the wilderness, proclaiming a baptism of repentance for the forgiveness of sins. And people from the whole Judean countryside and all the people of Jerusalem were going out to him, and were baptized by him in the river Jordan, confessing their sins. Now John was clothed with camel's hair, with a leather belt around his waist, and he ate locusts and wild honey. He proclaimed, 'The one who is more powerful than I is coming after me; I am not worthy to stoop down and untie the thong of his sandals. I have baptized you with water; but he will baptize you with the Holy Spirit.'

In those days Jesus came from Nazareth of Galilee and was baptized by John in the Jordan. And just as he was coming up out of the water, he saw the heavens torn apart and the Spirit descending like a dove on him. And a voice came from heaven, 'You are my Son, the Beloved; with you I am well pleased.'

Mark 1:4-11 (NRSV)

For those of us hoping to extend this season of good tidings and cheer just one more day, Mark's Gospel has a disappointing surprise for us. We find Jesus, not in a manger suckling at his mother's breast, nestled in soft bands of cloth, warm from the breath of the cows and sheep nearby, but standing waist deep in the muck of the Jordan, where so many of his ancestors—our too—had stood.

He had come there to be baptized by John. Now, John was a peculiar character in this story, someone we don't expect to be the first character we encounter in a Gospel. If you and I encountered someone who looked and acted like Mark's description of John on the street, we would surely cross to the other side. We might quietly admonish our children, "Don't stare, honey, it's impolite." And we might even consider calling the authorities if his calls for repentance were too loud or disturbing.

But many had come to John for the baptism he offered, and so did Jesus. And so our very first encounter of Jesus in this story is of him with John, coming up out of the water.

I never took swimming lessons as a child. My mother attempted to send me to some, but I was much too frightened and gave up after the first lesson. There was some overwhelming sense of the loss of control that water represented to me; it was a loss of control that I could not tolerate. My mother did not force me to learn. Because of my stubbornness I was doomed to a childhood of staying by the wall, holding on to the ladder, or merely dangling my feet in the water off the dock while other children splashed and swam and played "Marco Polo".

When it came time for me to be baptized (at the "age of accountability" that was the tradition in the faith community in which I was raised) I was terrified to find out that I would be baptized by immersion in the baptismal tank at church. Even worse, I would need to be fully immersed into the water not once, not twice, but three times.

When the day came, I climbed down the steps into three feet of very cold water, and my only words to the pastor were "Please don't let me drown." I had my breath taken from me three times that morning, and when I immerged from the water on the final dip, my only thought was not of the new beginning of my Christian life, or of having my sins washed away, or of the church, or of God really. It was that I had survived giving up the tiniest bit of control. I had never been all the way under water before—not since the womb.

It was a very un-Christ like thing Jesus had done that day, really. That the Savior for the world, Immanuel, God With Us, the Word Incarnate should come to John and submit to being submerged in the Jordan, that for those few seconds he should give up control and let the waters close over him, seems in some way unnecessary. He could have chosen another way. He didn't have to do it.

And yet, because he did, we have yet another mark of commonality with him. As he came up from the water to hear himself proclaimed aloud as God's own Beloved, so too are we.

When I finally did learn to swim it was liberating. The fear of loss of control eventually gave way to the sensation of being supported by something greater than myself, the knowledge that the water would not behave unpredictably, the satisfaction of knowing that the water and I could work in harmony, and at long last the feeling of safety in letting go.

May it be so for us in the Christian life. May this commemoration of the beginning of Jesus' ministry bring for us a fresh beginning in our own walk of devotion to the Triune God. May we feel supported, confident, harmonious and free to rely upon God as God's own beloved child each day.

Thanks be to God!

Loving, Supporting, Challenging God, we long for that sense of renewal and refreshment as we face the year ahead. Grant that we might find ways of submerging ourselves in your love each day. Amen.

Revmom/Cheesehead

January 9

He was in the world, and the world came into being through him; yet the world did not know him. He came to what was his own, and his own people did not accept him. But to all who received him, who believed in his name, he gave power to become children of God, who were born, not of blood or of the will of the flesh or of the will of man, but of God. And the Word became flesh and lived among us, and we have seen his glory, the glory as of a father's only son, full of grace and truth.

(John testified to him and cried out, 'This was he of whom I said, "He who comes after me ranks ahead of me because he was before me."') From his fullness we have all received, grace upon grace. The law indeed was given through Moses; grace and truth came through Jesus Christ. No one has ever seen God. It is God the only Son, who is close to the Father's heart, who has made him known. No one has ever seen God. It is God the only Son, who is close to the Father's heart, who has made him known.

John 1: 10-18 (NRSV)

No one has ever seen God. It is God the only Son, who is close to the Father's heart, who has made him known.

The Son is close to the Father's heart. A sweet expression of intimacy and love. One is not without the other. They are intertwined.

As Christmas season starts to close what we see are different things. What I see as the red thread throughout all of Christmas season is intimacy. The intimacy of the mother and her husband and their first born, her baby boy. The intimacy of the Father and the Son. And most amazingly the intimacy that is revealed to the world in Christ. God becoming mortal. God being born as a tiny baby in need of care, affection, love. God becoming one with human kind. God could not really get more intimate with us, could he?

From the intimacy of the Father and the Son— some theologians think— the Holy Spirit is born. It is as if the love that flows between the Father and the Son is so powerful and so all encompassing that it cannot just stay between the two. And, thus, the Holy Spirit rushes into the world to fill the hearts of humans. So that not only the Son is close to the Father's heart but we are, too. God is no longer somewhere outside of us but in us. In our heart. Just like we are and always were in His heart.

In the baptism of Jesus the three are present at the same time. The Father's voice, the Son standing in the water and the Holy Spirit descending like a dove. It is such a powerful image with heavens torn a part. At the same time the most touching aspect in it is what could be seen as the Father's desire to quite simply show off His Son.

We like to get other's attention to those things that are important to us in our lives. More so many of us really do like to show off those in our lives we love. We are proud of them and rejoice about every good deed, performance and aspect they have. Although it may seem more of a human response than godly I am not at all sure that it is not also a part of the way God loves. It is not bragging rather it is as if He says: "Look, is He not beautiful? Is He not wonderful? My Son. The apple of my eye."

This is also the "job" of the Holy Spirit. Quite simply to show off the Son. Not to brag but to bring to the forefront how Christ is. To teach about Him. To gently nudge us so that we lift our eyes to the Messiah. The Spirit does not even have His own name because it is the Son He wants to reveal to us, not himself. Now is not that God showing off His beautiful boy? As we should when it comes to the wonderful aspects of our loved ones and most importantly our God. And the amazing thing is it is not only the Son that God wants to show off. It is you and I. Daughters and sons of God. All of us the apple of His eye. A source of pride to Him. True and loving pride.

Father, Son and Holy Spirit,
You are three and one.
It is too amazing for us to understand.
In our baptism you have given us the power
    to become your children.
We are your beloved children and it is amazing to us.
Fill us with your love
    so that we too may know that we are close to your heart.
Let your Spirit be our guide in all of our lives. Amen.

Mia

January 10

Now every year his parents went to Jerusalem for the festival of the Passover. And when he was twelve years old, they went up as usual for the festival. When the festival was ended and they started to return, the boy Jesus stayed behind in Jerusalem, but his parents did not know it. Assuming that he was in the group of travelers, they went a day's journey. Then they started to look for him among their relatives and friends. When they did not find him, they returned to Jerusalem to search for him. After three days they found him in the temple, sitting among the teachers, listening to them and asking them questions. And all who heard him were amazed at his understanding and his answers. When his parents saw him they were astonished; and his mother said to him, 'Child, why have you treated us like this? Look, your father and I have been searching for you in great anxiety.' He said to them, 'Why were you searching for me? Did you not know that I must be in my Father's house?' But they did not understand what he said to them. Then he went down with them and came to Nazareth, and was obedient to them. His mother treasured all these things in her heart. And Jesus increased in wisdom and in years, and in divine and human favor.

Luke 2:41-52 (NRSV)

With this last meditation, we enter into the season after Epiphany, what some traditions term *Ordinary time*. It has no designation other than that, this space between Advent and Lent; it's really nothing more significant than the few weeks between the "real" seasons of Advent/Christmas and Lent/Easter. It's simply "in between" time.

And yet, as one of my favorite seminary professors would say, it's "more complicated than that." The two seasons, Advent and Lent, are certainly similar in many ways. They are periods of waiting, of preparation and transition. As I tell my young Christian Ed students, they are both *Getting Ready Times*. At the same time, they are also very different   One is a season of happy anticipation, the other one of somber introspection and dread. One is filled with transformative waiting, the other filled with transformative repentance.

Ordinary time, then, becomes significant. First it gives us some time off between all that focus and intentionality, and lets us relax a little. It allows us some chronological breathing space. Then it allows us the opportunity to recognize the differences, and to absorb the lessons from one so that we might better move into learning (and living) another. Sometimes the greatest truths become apparent only when we have room for perspective – looking back, then looking forward.

The reading for today illustrates this so very well. The only story we have of the boy Jesus is in this text of Luke. In one sense it is an old, familiar story: disobedient preteen meets irritated parents. The twelve-year-old Jesus is certainly old enough to go off on his own, and does; but he's also young and irresponsible enough that not turning up on schedule is cause for tracking him down in a mixture of anger and fear. I do not know a single parent, guardian or caregiver who has not at some point experienced that momentary panic, followed by an exasperated confrontation containing some variation on "What were you thinking??"   It's remarkable in its ordinary nature.

And yet...

This scene makes it obvious like nothing else that Mary and Joseph's baby boy is no longer a baby. He is not yet a man, but neither is he the dependent child who so needed their focus and vigilance. It was only a moment, and nothing visibly earth-shattering, really; but seeing him standing in the temple conversing with the priests like that must have been a startling flash of realization, as well as one of shocked relief. It would take some time for them to relax and absorb the perspective that moment showed them.

But the same moment that gave them that perspective, also offered a chance to move forward. Even as they were startled out of the past, they were shown the beginnings of the future. Their commitment to him remained whole and constant; but the way they lived that out would also need to change, and they would require some preparation for those changes.

By God's good favor, they had time, as *he increased in wisdom and in years, and in divine and human favor.* And Mary used that time well, *treasuring these things in her heart.*

We are also given that opportunity. As we slip off into Ordinary Time, it is with more of a whimper than a bang. A quiet, nondescript space that gives us room to grow into the earth-shattering, life-altering love and sacrifice we are offered. We needn't run off right away; we can stay in the temple quizzing each other, seeking answers and understanding. And then, like Mary, we can gather these things to treasure in our heart and move forward, knowing that though we don't see how or when or why, they will be needed in the time to come.

Lord, in the small and ordinary things of this life let us grow, move forward and sow and reap your love. A baby in a manger is indeed a small, ordinary thing. But through this small ordinary baby you have brought great and glorious things into the world. Let us always grow in love. In and of ourselves we cannot do great things – but you can help us do small ordinary things in great love. Help us to always hold the Baby close to our hearts and treasure the light that his birth has brought into our dark and broken world. *We know that the whole creation has been groaning in labor pains until now; and not only the creation, but we ourselves, who have the first fruits of the Spirit, groan inwardly while we wait for adoption, the redemption of our bodies*[22]. **We wait in hope, sometimes patient, sometimes not. Fill us with your light and love and grace. Help us to grow in faith and in faithfulness. In Christ blessed and holy name we pray. Amen.**

Jane Ellen and reverend mommy

---

[22] Romans 8:22-23 (NRSV)

Amy Avery Amy Avery writes the blog *Welcome to the Zoo* at http://www.amyavery.blogspot.com/. She writes "I'm a 25 year old single female who just graduated with a M.Div. from Western seminary in Holland, MI. I am currently pursuing my MSW degree at Western Michigan University in hopes that this degree will give me some greater experience and foundations for my future as a pastoral counselor. I have a deep passion and a calling to be with people in their pain and to help them work through life's most difficult times...realizing that hope, grace and growth are evident."

Ann http://yourcomfort.blogspot.com/ Ann Kansfield blogs at *What is your only comfort?: Urban Godtalk for the Church-O-Phobic* and serves as the pastor of the Greenpoint Reformed Church in Brooklyn, NY. She calls herself a "stand up theologizer" and says, "My life is a combination of "Archie Bunker" meets "Amen" but in a reality TV kind of way." Ann is honored to provide this goofie photo taken inside a tacky tourist shop in New Orleans last January. She and her partner Jennifer are currently hosting a Katrina evacuee in the spare room of their apartment.

Apstraight Apstraight is not a blogger but considers herself to be an important part of the community nonetheless, for she is one of those that reads and responds. Pastor of the Greencastle Presbyterian Church in Greencastle, PA she is one of many who juggles (sometimes successfully and sometimes not) being mother, wife, and pastor. "Every child should know love the way my daughter is loved by this church. It should be a birthright- not a privilege." This community of bloggers reminds her that she is one of many mother-wife-pastor combos.

Auntie Em http://aunt-em.blogspot.com/. Auntie Em blogs at *No Place Like Home* at. She says, "I'm seeking my role in Ministry in the United Methodist Church. Finding some interesting friends along the path." Auntie Em also writes, "Why a blog? I'm journaling like crazy right now. Any of the rest of the bloggers out there find themselves doing what I did? When I chose just the right journal book...nice cover...well-spaced lines...looks like the kind of book I need to use to fill with thoughts of this journey into Ministry in the United Methodist Church at the ripe old age of 61. Then I started writing. Oh, what a pretty first page. Then all hell broke loose. It's not a pretty sight now. I suppose I needed to get rid of all that garbage so that I would have room for other things in my heart, and around my soul." Auntie Em lives in Tennessee.

Cats http://findingavalon3.blogspot.com/ Christine Nessel can be found at *Finding Avalon*. She writes, "Who am I? Don't you just hate that question? I am... a woman, wife, mother, daughter, sister, friend, pastor, believer, sometimes crazy, and chocolate lover."

ChicagoRev/NotShyChiRev is the pastor of a small protestant congregation in Chicago, Illinois. Born and raised Southern Baptist in Houston, Texas, he left that denomination shortly after law school. A former litigator and appellate lawyer, he responded to a call to ministry that did not fully reveal itself until he accepted and understood himself to be gay. In what little spare time a solo pastorate allows him, he sings in a local civic chorus and the Chicago Gay Men's Chorus and reads voraciously. He is thrilled to be a chromosomally diverse member of RevGalBlogPals You can find *NotShyChiRev* at the blog http://www.journalscape.com/NotShyChiRev.

Emily Emily Schnabl writes "I am an Episcopal priest, wife, staff to two cats, rebeginning crocheter, very beginning knitter, reader, hiker, traveler, and ENFP." Emily lives in Oklahoma City and the name of her blog comes from her favorite Julian of Norwich quote: "And in this the Lord showed me something small, no bigger than a hazelnut, lying in the palm of my hand. In this little thing I saw three properties. The first is that God made it, the second is that God loves it, the third is that God preserves it." She blogs at *Hazelnut Reflections* found at http://hazelnutreflections.blogspot.com/.

Gallycat   Helen Thompson is an essayist and journalist who covers topics of faith for *The Philadelphia City Paper*, Crossleft.org, and just about anyone else who will let her write about her quirky relationship with God. She has enrolled in Education for Ministry through the Episcopal Church, and will head back to graduate school to study theology just as soon as she can pay for it. She lives in Fairfax, Va., with her fiancé, Dean, her son, Kieran, several very large plants, and a cat who likes to eat them. She blogs at http://gallycat.livejournal.com.

HeyJules   Hey Jules lives in Kansas City Missouri. She blogs at *Faith or Fiction* at http://www.faithorfiction.blogspot.com. She questions, "What holds me back from really digging in to Christianity? Do I really believe what the Bible says? Is remaining a Lutheran (what my parents taught me about religion) really the right path for me now that I am an adult? Do I need church to feel complete in my faith? If so, which denomination and which church? How do I feel about the life and death of Jesus? About reincarnation? About sin and forgiveness? How exactly does one turn their life over to God? What does that mean and how does it happen? ... So let's drop the attitude, open up our minds to something new and see what happens."

Jane Ellen   Jane Schmoetzer blogs at *Hoosier Musings on the Road to Emmaus,* found at http://janellen.blogspot.com. There she posts "thoughts, observations, and the occasional sermon from a wife, mother, and Episcopal priest." A former steelmaker (her undergraduate degree is in Metallurgical Engineering), stay-at-home mom and substitute teacher, she currently serves as the assistant pastor at St. Andrew's by the Lake Episcopal Church in Michigan City, Indiana.

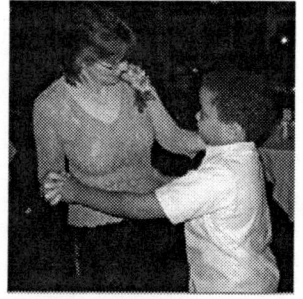

Jennifer Jennifer Spreng of *Ordinary Time* was brought up in the Unitarian Universalist tradition and became a Christian when she was 12. She recently graduated from college where she studied history and sociology. She is in her first year of seminary in the Northeast and hopes to be ordained in the Episcopal Church following her graduation. Meanwhile, her blog is http://ordinarytime.blogspot.com.

Jenee Jenee Woodard writes and blogs at *Textweek Blog* found at http://textweek.blogs.com/textweek/. She describes her blog as "study, preaching, & worship resources, links & thoughts." Many more people are familiar with her main website http://www.textweek.com which is an extraordinary collection of resources for Scripture study, worship and liturgy links and resources, indexed according to the texts of the Revised Common Lectionary. It is the premier website for preachers, pastors and scholars for research as it is not limited to one particular ideology, but contains a huge and diverse range of material.

Katherine Katherine E. W. Pershey posts her musings at *any day a beautiful change* (http://www.kewp.blogspot.com). In May 2005, she was ordained as a minister in the Christian Church (Disciples of Christ), and was soon after called to serve South Bay Christian Church of Redondo Beach, CA as a solo pastor. Katherine's favorite ministerial activities include preaching, developing meaningful relationships with congregants, and encouraging people to grow and share their faith. She and her husband, Benjamin, share an enthusiasm for good coffee, alt-country music, the *LA Times*, and an adopted mutt named Deacon.

Kathryn Kathryn blogs at *Good in Parts* found at http://www.goodinparts.blogspot.com/. She says "Just settling into the reality of full-time Anglican ministry, after 10 years of part-timing as a Reader. I'm Mum of 3 teenagers, who are kind enough to believe that I love them passionately despite the frequent interruptions to family life. I've been married for nearly 20 years now to a long-suffering clock-maker, who is a dab hand at tuna pasta and instant artifacts. I'm a chronic procrastinator, always up for some displacement activity online or anywhere else, until the blessed Deadline looms. The typical prayer for my Myers Briggs type runs something like 'Lord, help me to concentrate on just one— oh look, a bird!— thing at a time' which just about says it all." Kathryn lives in Gloucestershire, UK.

Lorna Lorna blogs at *see through faith* found at http://stf.heavenlytrain.com/. She writes "I live in Finland, though I am English. I am 45 and my husband and I have two teenage children as well as a young golden retriever who loves everyone and is the best evangelist in our family. I am a member and local preacher in the United Methodist Church and have just become a candidate for ordination. I'm currently studying theology at the seminary in Tallinn, Estonia and hope to graduate in 2008."

Lutheran Chik Lutheran Chik blogs at *LutheranChik's 'L' Word Diary* found at http://lutheranchiklworddiary.blogspot.com/. She asks, "Can a liturgically minded, lectionary-loving, link-collecting ELCA Lutheran laywoman find happiness and kindred spirits on the Internet? Ja, you betcha! 'Here I blog; I can do no other; God help me.' *Soli Deo gloria*!" Lutheran Chik lives somewhere in Michigan. LutheranChik's midlife crisis led her to a new adventure as a newbie enrollee in the lay ministry training program of her ELCA synod. She's recently facilitated short-term online discussion groups on Praying the Daily Office and *lectio divina,* and has a keen interest in exploring ways to do ministry on the Internet. She also works in the nonprofit sector, doing community outreach and volunteer recruitment. She attends a little white-clapboard church next to a hayfield, in a community so remote that in order to find it you pretty much have to be lost to begin with. When not blogging, she enjoys walking, birding, gardening, art-fair-ing, reading, music and cooking.

Mary Beth Mary Beth Butler is an Episcopal laywoman, choir member, Lay Eucharistic Visitor and Daughter of the King. She works in international education at a north Texas university and blogs at *Terrapin Station*: http://www.marybethbutler.typepad.com. She and her husband also own and run a parking-lot striping company, and their 16 year-old son and 3 year-old Maltese keep them laughing (mostly).

Mia Mia Wittaniemi is a priest in the Evangelical Lutheran Church of Finland. Her congregation is English speaking and they celebrate a Eucharistic service every Sunday at 4pm in the chapel in Turku cathedral. (The third Sunday of each month is an Anglican service). There is also Evensong once a fortnight on Thursdays. She sings soprano in the choir, and one of their specialities is singing the psalms, which Mia loves. She also serves as the university chaplain for Turku University and the local School of Economics. She does not blog, but is a staunch supporter of the RevGalBlogPal community.

Mibi Mary Brennan Thorpe writes and blogs at *Rev-to-be-Mibi* found at http://rev2bmibi.blogspot.com/. She describes herself as "a middle-aged banking exec in the neighborhood of Your Nation's Capitol. I'm married to Pastoral Husband (otherwise known as PH), who is a pastoral counselor. I am in the midst of the discernment process to become an Episcopal priest, hoping to go to seminary in August 2006."

Pink Shoes Pink Shoes blogs at *Pink Shoes in the Pulpit* found at http://preacherinpink.blogspot.com/. "For now, it's all about the shoes and the pulpit. Well, and a few other things added in for good measure."

Purechristianithink Purechristianithink blogs at *Rebel Without A Pew* found at http://rebelwithoutapew.blogspot.com/. "Does climbing into the pulpit week after week give a girl a skewed, unrealistic view of reality? Absolutely! Read all about it . . ."

Quotidian Grace Jody Harrington blogs at *Quotidian Grace* (Daily Grace) found at http://www.quotidiangrace.blogspot.com/. A former attorney and stay-at-home mom, she spent many years as a church and community volunteer and currently is Director of Christian Education in a Presbyterian Church (USA) near Houston, Texas.

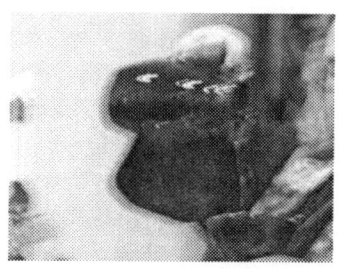

reverend mommy Theresa Coleman blogs, writes and posts her photography at *reverend mommy's random thoughts* at http://reverendmommy.blogspot.com/. She writes, "I'm a perpetual student at Emory University's Candler School of Theology (I have 5 years of post-graduate schooling — ack!) and will finish with my education just in time to move into assisted living. I am the Minister of Christian Education at Grayson United Methodist Church just outside of Atlanta Georgia. I am a wife and a mother of two beautiful girls 9 and 11, who I call (to the amusement of the Loving Husband) Chaos and Entropy."

reverendmother is a minister in the Presbyterian Church (USA), a writer, and a knitter of splendidly imperfect projects. Her weblog (at www.reverendmother.org) deals with her adventures in pastoring and parenting. She lives in the mid-Atlantic region with her husband and daughter. They are expecting another daughter in late December, which means that reverendmother is pondering Mary's Advent journey once again this year.

Revmom/Cheesehead Revmom/Cheesehead blogs, writes and ponders life at http://www.journalscape.com/cheesehead. She says, "As a seasoned marriage partner of over 20 years, and an experienced Mom to two nearly-grown children, I was quite surprised (delighted is too strong a word) to find my career in women's reproductive health care interrupted by God's call to ordained ministry. But here I am: Midwestern, Mainline, Middle-aged, and Ministering. This blog is a place for me to ponder parentally, think theologically, and in general express my wonder at this marvelous thing called life. (With the occasional poem thrown in for good measure.)"

revstacey revstacey blogs at *thoughts from a first-year minister* found at http://www.firstyearminister.blogspot.com/. She writes, "I'm a minister, just arrived in my first congregation, and thus writing mostly about that unusual experience."

Smallest Angel Carol McKay is the Associate Pastor of a United Methodist Church in downtown Huntington, WV. Among her many ministries, she enjoys reaching out to college students; leading the worship team for Common Grounds, a contemporary service; and working with youth and adults in Bible studies. Before answering the call to full-time ministry, Carol taught math to youth in middle school and high school as well as adults. In her spare time, she loves to play with her four year old son, Jake. Carol blogs at http://www.smallestangel.blogspot.com.

Songbird Songbird blogs at *Set Free* found at http://revsongbird.typepad.com/set_free. A native of Virginia, she pastors a small United Church of Christ congregation in Maine, parents three precocious sermon critics, pets two Bernese Mountain Dogs and three Refuge League cats, and ponders the unanswerable questions with her long-suffering, long-distance hiker husband.

InnerDorothy Sue at *InnerDorothy* is a dreamer, stumbling along the life's path looking for glimpses of holiness. She is deeply blessed to be sharing that path with genuinely good people, including her partner of twenty-five years, her sons, and a few good cats. She shares her ministry with a United Church of Canada congregation, and enjoys writing, laughing, reading and chocolate. She believes in the magical and mystical power of words. You can find her at http://innerdorothy.blogspot.com/.

Susan Rose Susan Rose Francois is a candidate for vowed membership with the Sisters of St. Joseph of Peace, a Roman Catholic congregation of women religious. She is documenting her journey on her blog, *Musings of a Discerning Woman* at http://www.actjustly.blogspot.com. She writes, "I'm a recovering bureaucrat who's finding a way to do what she's really called to do and follow that Jesus guy instead of creating red tape."

Susie Susie Shaefer is an Episcopal priest who keeps track of songs, sermons and such at her blog *Nueva Cantora: A New Song* (http://nuevacantora.blogspot.com). Her days are filled with Church School and sermon preparation, cooking shows, football, and walking with her husband Luke. She is in her first year of ordained ministry, and is still sorting out what the soundtrack of this part of her life will sound like, but she always has a song stuck in her head.

Steph Stephanie Youstra, OSB, is a Sister of Saint Benedict of Ferdinand, Indiana. Although she entered the community three years ago, she still occasionally faces the culture shock of small-town rural life, and still isn't quite used to being called "Sister." Originally from the Washington, DC, metropolitan area, Steph shares her Benedictine journey (and other not-so-related thoughts) on *Narrow at the Outset* at http://nuntime.blogspot.com. Her official full-time ministry involves teaching New Testament and Social Justice at a Catholic girls high school in Louisville; her part-time pursuits include music, photography, creating silly songs, outdoorsy stuff, keeping people at the monastery on their toes, procrastinating, causing good-natured trouble, and avoiding cleaning her room. As a spiritual klutz, she ensures for herself plenty of

practice at the "getting up" phase of the spiritual journey, and appreciates the encouragement of the RevGalBlogPals.

terri c terri c blogs at *Ps 121 is my Friend*, http://www.ps121ismyfriend.blogspot.com/."Older, shorter, rounder than I might wish. Returning to school after a long time working in the computer industry, to fulfill a dream. Pinching self often. Love to laugh, love to make people laugh. Gentle, nonconforming, questioning, thoughtful, profoundly silly."

will smama Will Smama is an ordained minister in the Presbyterian Church (USA) and is currently serving as solo pastor with a congregation in central, rural Pennsylvania. Blogging is a recent hobby made all the better for the community of women she has become a part of online. She and her husband have a son who is almost one year old. Her blog can be found at *Preacher, Blogger or Procrastinator* at: www.preacherbloggerorprocrastinator.blogspot.com

Printed in the United States
129265LV00002B/107/A